A FAMILY SECRET

T0083519

A FAMILY SECRET
AND OTHER STORIES

BIJOYA SAWIAN

zubaan

Zubaan
an imprint of Kali for Women
128b Shahpur Jat, 1st floor
New Delhi 110 049
Email: contact@zubaanbooks.com
Website: www.zubaanbooks.com

First published by Zubaan 2014

10 9 8 7 6 5 4 3 2 1

ISBN: 978-93-83074-06-8

Zubaan is an independent feminist publishing house based in New Delhi with a strong academic and general list. It was set up as an imprint of India's first feminist publishing house, Kali for Women, and carries forward Kali's tradition of publishing world quality books to high editorial and production standards. *Zubaan* means tongue, voice, language, speech in Hindustani. Zubaan is a non-profit publisher, working in the areas of the humanities, social sciences, as well as in fiction, general non-fiction, and books for children and young adults under its Young Zubaan imprint.

Typeset in Sabon Lt Std 11/13.8 by Jojy Philip
Printed at Raj Press, R-3 Inderpuri, New Delhi 110 012

for
my parents and Anjalika

CONTENTS

ACKNOWLEDGEMENTS

Many thanks to Neena De and Udita Bhargava for going through the stories and for their valuable suggestions. I would also like to thank Rati Singh for the cover photograph and Devika Choudhury for her evocative cover design.

Preeti Gill and Anita Roy of Zubaan for their support, and the tellers of the stories who came over mountains and valleys and mighty rivers to relate their secret moments "spinning out of nothingness scattering stars like dust." (Rumi).

SAPHIRA
A FAMILY SECRET

She was fourteen and studying at the Ramakrishna Mission School in Sohra, a pretty town known worldwide as Cherrapunjee, the wettest place on earth. She was only too happy to miss school on that cold, end-of-February morning. She listened to the school bell ring for morning assembly and slid happily back into the warmth of her quilt. Very soon she fell asleep, no longer feverish but still weak.

She had developed a cough and cold during the usual Sunday outing at Sderkariah when clothes were washed in the stream and spread out on the rocks to dry followed by a sumptuous lunch cooked *al fresco*. Of course, there was no reason for her to catch a cold on that unusually sunny morning except that Saphira had slipped and fallen into the stream while fetching water for the men and women who were cooking. The water was freezing and she had shivered, her teeth chattering, while she changed behind a big rock. Her father wisely suggested that she take a spoonful of brandy from his stock but her mother and aunts objected most vociferously although most of them were certainly not teetotalers. So that was the end of that. She was served hot chicken soup and made to sleep in the sun with an umbrella as sunshade. She had a good lunch but by the time she reached home she had fever. The next morning her cough surfaced and and her nose ran like a tap. "How weak she has become," commented her grandmother. She didn't know that that wasn't the real reason for her granddaughter falling ill. She fell ill because she was about to discover a family secret.

So she was at home that Wednesday at eleven o'clock when the letter arrived for her aunt, Lanalin Dohling. After making sure that there were no dogs around a man opened the gate and stepped inside. "No letter box around here?" he hollered. Saphira shook her head.

Postmen were as rare a sight as a swallow on a winter's day. Since her mother's family owned two buses besides the bakery, letters for the family arrived via the bus drivers. They were always obliging, enjoying the smiles that the letters would, inevitably, bring to the grateful, expectant faces. So in the small, far-flung towns of Meghalaya, this was and is the fastest form of communication. To Saphira's house the letters that came were mostly from Shillong where many of the relatives lived. A few resided in the smaller towns along the way, Mylliem, Mawjrong, Mawkdok, Sohrarim, Laitryngew. One uncle lived in Nongstoin, in West Khasi Hills. Everyone in Sohra felt rather sorry that marriage, a love marriage, had taken him to the 'wild west'. For the people of Sohra, rightly or not, proud of their renowned etiquette, polished manner of speech and refined features, looked upon this alliance as not quite appropriate.

The postman smiled and handed the letter to Saphira, His face was familiar like everyone else's in this small town. If her grandmother had been there she would have made customary small talk and asked him how things were with him and his family, what clan he belonged to and where he lived after which she would have served him kwai. Saphira, on the other hand, could barely whisper khublei for she was staring at the envelope, totally absorbed.

The postmark clearly read "Chandigarh" circling the leopard-cat stamp that sat on the right hand corner. Saphira studied the envelope – the handwriting, the stamp, the texture, stroking its creamy white surface with childish awe. Even Archies envelopes weren't quite like this one and it had come all the way from Chandigarh! At least she knew where it was and felt satisfied and erudite. Yet who could have written this letter to her youngest aunt in a neat, yet distinctly masculine hand? That she could not fathom. So she resorted to what she always did when such situations arose: she would go and ask an elder. Her father had gone down to Mawmluh where he worked in the cement factory. Her mother and aunt were at the bakery, which was too far to walk to considering she had fever. Only her grandmother was at home, in her room at the other end of the house. Since she was not well she could have sent the letter through Rinsi the maid but she did not want Rinsi to have the pleasure of delivering such an important letter. Besides she wanted to know who could have written to her aunt from far away Chandigarh.

Saphira somehow knew that it wasn't just any letter and she wanted to star in it from the beginning of its story. She placed her little hand on her chest and sighed with relief that she was actually at home on that week-day morning. She gazed admiringly at the envelope again. The handwriting was totally unfamiliar as was the colour and shape of the envelope with the sweet-faced leopard cat on the five-rupee stamp.

The room in the eastern corner of the house, with the two big Godrej almirahs and the five tin trunks stacked in one corner, was fairly large. In fact, it was the largest room in the house, her Meirad's room. Kong Binola Dohling did not believe in banks and in keeping her money with anyone but herself, under her watchful eye. That had something to do not only with her youngest daughter's unfortunate experiences but more with her own. She despised banks ever since her first cheque bounced because the signatures did not match. She had sent the cheque to her favourite nephew in Shillong when he graduated with distinction. She told no one when she signed it with a flourish after filling in "one thousand only" and sent it through a cousin who had come visiting. Imagine the horror and humiliation she felt when the unthinkable happened! "What do you mean the signatures do not match? *This* is *my* signature so is *that* and that's that." She listened to no explanation and withdrew the entire amount she had and closed her account. At home she threw all her bank papers into the dustbin. "How can they question my integrity? Nobody in my family has cheated in a thousand years."

"It is to protect your interest, Mei" cajoled Daphira, Saphira's mother, the eldest of the Dohlings but her words fell on deaf ears. Hence the two Godrej almirahs and five tin trunks in her room contained all her cash, clothes and her entire collection of gold, silver and coral jewellery, silks, velvets and brocades. Kong Binola Dohling did not like chairs so mulas, cane stools, stood obediently against the wall, ready for use. When Saphira burst into her room she was sitting on an extra large one and at her feet was Rinsi, the maid, deep in concentration over her embroidery.

"Meirad, there's a letter for Nah Duh," Saphira gushed.

"Really? Put it in her room, Saphi, and how are you feeling darling?"

"Oh! Meirad ... " Saphira began but her grandmother had already gone back to Rinsi's work. She took these classes very seriously and was very proud that she had taught more than a dozen girls who had worked for her and who went on to do her proud. Otherwise Saphira, the only granddaughter of Binola Dohling was never ignored by her grandmother or anyone in the household. Saphira knew that this moment in her grandmother's day had an unwritten "Do Not Disturb" sign. But then today was not just any day.

"Meirad, this letter is from Chandigarh," she announced bravely.

Her grandmother's looked up from the sea-green tablecloth Rinsi was working on and stared at the wall ahead. Saphira could feel the atmosphere getting tense and it startled her. The envelope dropped from her hand and sailed down to her grandmother's feet.

"Oh dear! It'll get dirty," Saphira cried out.

"Pick it up Saphi and put it in Nah Duh's room." whispered Kong Binola Dohling quietly moving her foot away. Rinsi simply looked up and stared at Saphira.

Saphira, aged fourteen, understood the tone. She knew that she shouldn't utter another word and that she should do what she was told. So that was exactly what she did after which she went to the kitchen and asked Thei, the cook, to give her an early lunch. As she was eating her fish curry and rice and a plate of salad of crisp cucumber and fresh tangy tomatoes, Rinsi walked in with a glass of water and half a paracetamol.

"Meirad said please have this after your lunch. She is tired and she is resting," Rinsi explained almost apologetically.

Saphira continued to eat, far too bewildered to respond. She turned to the elderly Thei wanting to ask so many questions but heard herself asking how come there was no pork dish on the table and was told that one did not eat pork when one had fever. She was also told that she could have a cream bun with either lemon tea or Horlicks when she woke up from her sleep and that Rinsi would bring it to her. She did not have a clue about Saphi's dinner but she, personally, suggested a chicken stew or just soup if the fever persisted. Saphira listened politely to the domestic help as all well-brought-up Sohra girls did but her mind was totally occupied by the cream envelope that the postman had delivered that morning. Intrigued and perplexed especially by her Meirad's reaction she dragged herself to her room and fell asleep.

When she woke up it was past four o'clock, a couple of minutes away from dusk in the eastern town. She could hear homing birds chirping sleepily as they winged their way back to their nests. She heard other noises too – many people talking in low tones like the murmurs of hill streams. As she strained to listen, she noticed that her curtains had been drawn and the zero power bulb attached to the switchboard was on. A mug of Horlicks and a cream bun were on her bedside table. She knew it was her grandmother's way of showing concern and Saphira smiled, contented. The hum of so many voices, however, continued to puzzle her. The voices were getting louder and louder as the minutes ticked away.

Saphira was feeling too weak to move. Her Meirad's reaction to the letter had unsettled her and now the voices.

Amidst that din she longed to hear the reassuring voice of her father. She felt so helpless. Something must have happened. She was certain of that. Her parents were occupied and thought she was asleep. "Mei, Pa" she cried out soundlessly and shutting her eyes tight she tried to think. Her father stood there smiling, framed in the doorway. He was always like that: a smile on his lips and love in his eyes.

Saphira sprang out of bed and out of sheer relief tears welled up in her eyes.

"Pa!"

"How are you? How's my child?"

He hugged her tight. She kissed him on both cheeks as tears streamed down her cheeks.

"All right, all right. Now let's see if your smile is wider than mine? No? Okay, at least open your mouth wide and let me check your throat ... Your throat still needs care ... "

"Pa!"

"Yes?"

"Why have so many people come to the house?"

"Not so many, Saphi. Just a few ... ten, twelve in all."

"Pa, it's not every day that we get twelve visitors on a week-day."

"Hmm … "

"Pa, is it, is it … Pa today Nah Duh received a letter from Chandigarh. Don't look so shocked. I know because the postman handed the letter to me."

"Hmn … "

"What is it Pa? Good news, bad news?"

"Hmn … both. Oh! I don't know Saphi. Let me ask your Mei to come and speak with you. She came in twice earlier but you were fast asleep. Relax now. I'll just send you another cup of Horlicks. Do you want anything else darling?"

"No! Just Mei, please. Please send her."

Saphira sat up on her bed and tried to listen to the voices. She knew she was doing something wrong, eavesdropping like that, so she was grateful that she heard nothing. She slid back inside her quilt and tried to sleep. Not very long after, her mother arrived and gathered Saphi in her arms. She then sat down on the bed, holding her daughter close.

"Why Mei? Why are there so many people in the house?"

"Saphi, it's about your Nah Duh. You see she was married to a Sikh gentleman named Baljit Singh. After just four years of marriage, of a very happy marriage, he passed away in his ancestral home not far from Chandigarh. He had gone there on a visit."

"How did he die? Poor Nah Duh, was she there?"

"He, he … died of a heart attack. No, Nah Duh wasn't there. He had gone alone on some work." Her mother raced through her words sounding decidedly uncomfortable but Saphira was too intrigued to give up.

"The letter?"

"The letter received today was from his younger brother, Sukhjit Singh. He … "

"Yes, what did he write?"

"My baby you are so inquisitive!"

"Naturally Mei, I received the letter. The postman walked in and gave it to ME and I put it in Nah Duh's room."

"I know. Well your late Pakhynnah's brother has written that the family property matters have been settled and he wants to come and give Nah Duh's share."

"Oh! *Issh*! How wonderful! I do remember Pakhynnah vaguely."

"You do? You were very little, maybe four years old."

"So have the relatives come to congratulate Nah Duh?"

"No, Saphi."

"Why?"

"Because Nah Duh says that she doesn't want a single paisa. So Ma Rangbah and Ma Thomlin are here along with your Pakhynnah Teibor, he's a lawyer you know."

Saphi found herself sighing with relief. The very thought of the presence of both her maternal uncles and her father's brother made her feel secure.

"They will sort out everything Mei. Don't look so worried, but why is Nah Duh not taking her share?"

Her mother pursed her lips and cast her eyes downwards and was silent.

"Is it a secret, Mei?"

Her mother did not answer but the silence spoke volumes. Saphi kept looking at her mother, her curiosity increasing with every breath, as the elder shifted uncomfortably.

"Then?" Saphira persisted.

"It's not a secret, child. She … just wants only what he

really liked and nothing more. She knew he had collected some beautiful pieces of furniture which were lying in his ancestral home."

"Nah Duh doesn't want anything more?"

"No, Saphi, no. Now you will ask me why. Well, she attended her husband's funeral along with ... along with ... Ma Thomlin and our cousin, your San Ginia who lives in Delhi. When she returned she decided ... well she decided that she doesn't want to be part of his family anymore. He was gone so what was the point, no? She even threw away the cheques that were sent to her. She wanted nothing of the past."

"Is it that or is there a secret reason Mei?"

Daphira Dohling stared at her daughter, wide-eyed, startled. Then she quickly said, "I'll send your dinner. Read a bit, you can't watch TV today. There are too many people in the drawing room... I will send Rinsi to sit with you."

"No, Mei, I will read," Saphi dared to lie because she wanted to be alone with her thoughts.

The visitors stayed late into the night. The discussion continued during dinner and during the customary serving of kwai afterwards and into late cups of red tea right up to midnight. Saphira drifted in and out of sleep trying hard to capture images of her late uncle from the northern plains of Punjab so far away. She was treated to one phone call in between from her cousin, Maphisha.

"Are they still there? Exciting isn't it?"

"I am confused, "

"What's so confusing? Some people have come from Punjab and we all have to be very dignified and correct about it all. This is what I figured."

"I see," responded Saphi in total agreement. All the cousins were in awe of Maphi because of her intelligence. Her mother, Miramai, equally beautiful and brilliant, was the daughter of a Bengali homeopath in Shillong. "*Khun dkhar te*" (she's a plainsman's daughter after all) they would all comment, whenever some commendable achievement was bestowed on Miramai in studies, dramatics and debates and other activities during her academic years.

The following morning Saphira extracted the information about the previous night's outcome from her father. She learnt that it had been decided by the elders of the family, chiefly her mother's eldest brother and her grandmother, that if it was some kind of charity nothing would be accepted. If what was being offered was truly a legitimate share of the late Baljit Singh's property then it would be put in a fixed deposit and the interest accrued would be used to pay for the education of a deserving child in the little village of Umroi where Baljit had planned to open a fruit-canning factory. It was pineapple country, that sleepy village, not far from Shillong. Baljit Singh had fallen in love with it on a visit to a relative's house built off a dusty offshoot of the main road where poultry strolled around casually and cats lazed in the sun. "We should not refuse the money if, indeed, it is truly his. It would be insulting and disrespectful and would belittle the memory of such a good man." The question of Baljit Singh's valuable antique furniture would be left entirely to Lanalin, because after all, it was a personal decision regarding the belongings of the husband she'd loved.

The reply was composed, read out to the rest of the family by Thomlin Dohling and written out in long hand by Bhiren Dohling, the eldest of the brothers. The visit was fixed for the last week of March to suit Sukhjit Singh's family. His children's holidays began then and continued for two weeks before they joined school in their new classes. The weather too would be perfect.

For days on end Saphi and her cousin planned what they were going to wear. They would certainly go to Shillong and shop. They must impress their relatives from Chandigarh. Other arrangements were organized by the adults: where the Sodhis would stay, what sightseeing they would do and the menus of course keeping in mind that it was the Sodhis first visit and would probably be their last.

The Sodhis arrived in a Sumo taxi on a windy March evening. It was the time for strong winds but that evening it was exceptionally so. Trees swayed and bent like vengeful witches and shook furiously as the last few leaves swirled to the ground and perished. The sky was not its normal inky hue but black with clouds that seemed heavy with secrets. Saphi thanked God that the lights had not gone off. Deep inside she felt a hidden fear.

The long drive from Guwahati to Cherrapunjee via Shillong had taken its toll on the visitors. Sukhjit Singh looked totally worn out as his family braved the wind, trying to smile and not being able to.

"He has really aged," Giginia Dohling remarked. "He looks as if he has just been discharged from the hospital." She had met him at the funeral in Chandigarh and taken an instant dislike to him.

"Welcome, welcome, Khublei," Bhiren Dohling was saying, extending both his hands and touching them in the traditional Khasi way.

Everyone around him, Thomlin and Teibor, Giginia Dohling and her husband Kynpham, Saphira and four of her cousins wished the Sodhis, 'Khublei', welcome, God bless you.

Saphira's mother glanced at her sister expecting her to say something but Lanalin Dohling had simply folded her hands and was staring at nobody in particular, looking but not seeing. So she cleared her throat and in her best English, said, "We are so happy you have come, welcome, khublei."

"We are happy too to be here. See we came straight to Cherra and didn't get tempted by Shillong!" replied Mrs Sukhjit Sodhi. Her lips, hurriedly coloured in the car, were smudged out of shape. "Sukhi thought we should get it over with … I mean meet his brother's … er … family … so nice, so nice really."

"We are happy to be here and thank you for your warm welcome," Sukhjit Singh intervened speaking slowly and firmly, silencing his wife's chatter.

It was already past six o'clock and it was cold and dark but nobody seemed to realize it. The whole group stood in the porch of the Circuit House looking dazed. Saphi was staring at her young relatives from Punjab when she saw Indra Sodhi hugging herself, braving the cold. Her father noticed it too and whispered to his brother-in-law. It was only then that Bhiren Dohling ushered the visitors indoors.

"Come in, come in. Why are we standing outside?" he said in his quiet, gentle manner, slightly embarrassed by the lapse on his part.

The sitting-cum-dining room of the Circuit House had been cleaned and aired and a glowing coal fire now warmed the large room. The booking had been done by a minister whose wife was from Cherra so there were flowers in the vases and a bowl of fruit on the table. Teiborlang, the younger brother of Giginia's husband, was basically a Sohra boy and would always remain so, yet when it came to whiskies he could beat a connoisseur. He developed a taste for the "elixir of life" as he called it, quite early. While he was in Shillong studying at St Anthony's College, he stayed with his aunt Kha Nora, his father's sister, and her English husband Tony Jenkins. A retired tea planter, Tony Jenkins taught Teibor to trim hedges and prune roses, to lay the correct cutlery on the dining table, to marinade beef and pork and to enjoy the best whisky. By the time he graduated and went on to join the Law College, he was famous for his bar. So in honour of the guests from the north he had requested a friend in Air India to bring him a bottle of Black Label, a single malt and two bottles of Chardonnay for the ladies, and cognac and Bailey's for after dinner.

"The time and weather is just right for a drink," he suggested, his eyes brightening with the thought of that first incomparable swig. Besides, he had found himself standing next to Lanalin and the way she quietly wrung her hands and stared at the carpet had unsettled him.

The men moved to one side of the room, away from the fire, to the corner where the glasses and the soda, water and ice had been readied. On the centre table a plate of finely cut carrots, cucumbers and radish along with slices of ham took pride of place. The ladies remained by the fireside and cups of tea were served to them along with patties and pastries and a glass of Chardonnay each for San Giginia and Indra Sodhi. The children had happily trundled off to the bedroom to chat and watch television looking forward to the forbidden fruits that had been carted down – Pepsis and Cokes, chips and hamburgers, chocolates and ice cream. By then Saphira had got over her disappointment at not being allowed to wear jeans and had settled for a deep red skirt with a matching jacket.

The Minister and his wife had driven down from Shillong especially to help out the Dohlings on that first evening. So the little party turned out to be a great success as the hot plates of fish cutlets and chicken tikkas made their rounds and were washed down happily with big gulps of whisky and wine.

It was nearing ten when the merriment broke up. Bhiren Dohling saw his sisters looking meaningfully at him and he understood. Lanalin had requested her brothers that she would like to leave before the meal. Everyone agreed to do so too. The Sodhis would have a quiet dinner on their own.

So the Dohlings and the Minister and his wife said their goodbyes and left. They were to meet again the following morning, after which there would be sightseeing and a picnic lunch. All seemed to be well, everyone seemed contented. Only Saphira sitting in her mother's lap in the back seat of the Sumo pretending to be asleep saw the unshed tears in her aunt's eyes. Like frozen ponds they shone, as the vehicle sped along the moon-washed road back to Sohra.

The following morning they found the Sodhis enjoying a sumptuous breakfast of fresh country eggs sunny side up on toasted brown bread, along with sausages and bacon and tall glasses of milk shake. After savouring a couple of cups of Lakyrsiew tea the men went inside the drawing room and the women sat in a circle in the sunlit lawn. Giginia Dohling, being a well-travelled woman because of her husband's job as a Central Service officer, regaled

Indra Sodhi with stories in her inimitable style. The best one was of her stay in Chandigarh, when she had a– as she put it – medical problem. She kept everyone in splits with her clever comments as they all tried to guess what the problem was, especially the truly fascinated Indra Sodhi.

"Uterus?"

"Trust you!

"Eyes?"

"Lies!"

"Tummy?"

"Yummy!"

In that light and joyous vein the women passed an hour in the sun. Even Lanalin smiled tenderly at her vivacious cousin, basking gratefully in the comfort of her *joie de vivre*. In the distance the children sat on the parapet and chatted animatedly, their legs dangling. Saphira sat at one end. Every now and then she would steal a glance at her Nah Duh and when she saw her smile she too would smile to herself, for no one else knew what she knew.

After an hour the men emerged looking calm as Sukhjit Singh wiped his forehead and put on his dark glasses. The women got up and slowly walked towards the men. There were no expectations and, therefore, no stress. Binola Dohling had told them all on the last family gathering before the Sodhis arrived, "Remember the honour of the family and our community is of utmost importance. Next to that is the memory of a son-in-law who gave me full respect and who I loved very much." And having uttered those few lines, in front of the stunned family, Binola shed a tear. That, in itself, conveyed a lot.

"What's the programme now?" asked Indra Sodhi

pulling down her Benetton sweat shirt, looking like an overweight starlet. "Sukhiji, you sit in the car, you will be more comfortable. You know he has osteoarthritis," she whispered to Giginia.

The three vehicles purred out of the gate of the Circuit House down the dark tarmac road, which coiled languidly to join the main road with its arterial roads to the towns of Cherrra and Shillong, southwards to the Bangladesh border and east and west to the villages and the waterfalls. The convoy of cars went past the Presbyterian Church, established in 1852, the oldest in Meghalaya. Soon after, they drove past the 'kpeps', the royal cremation ground of the Sohra kings. It was decided that the group would not visit the famous Mawsmai caves to see the stalactites and stalagmites because Sukhjit would not be able to walk on the uneven stones and rocks that crouch over the caves like goblins. So they carried on to the main Sohra town and to the spectacular waterfalls, Noh Ka Likai. As they walked they heard the roar of the water as it thundered down the cliffs to the rocks below.

According to legend the shattered Ka Likai had jumped to her death from the cliff down to the waterfalls when she accidentally discovered that her second husband, an insanely jealous man, had killed her beloved child, cooked her and fed the flesh to her. The story was related by Saphi's father. Indra Sodhi recoiled with horror and turning away said, "I don't know how any human being can commit such horrendous crimes". Lanalin watched her intently as if she was seeing someone for the first time.

As they all spilled out of the car, everyone noticed how difficult it was for Sukhjit Singh to be elegant in spite of his élan and distinguished looks. He was visibly shaken by the

story of the falls and that worsened his gait. Giginia, Indra
Sodhi and Saphira watched him as he limped alongside the
rest of the men; they watched him too.

It was only much later when they were lunching at Thang
Kharang, gazing at the plains of Bangladesh below that
Giginia sat next to Sukhjit and inquired, "What medication
are you talking for your aches and stiffness?"

"Just herbal oil massages and an occasional pain killer,"
he replied, eyeing her quizzically. He was always wary of
Ginia.

"I don't know why it happened. He eats so sensibly,
he is so active, he supervises all the work in the farms and
plays golf as well," moaned Indra Sodhi.

"Yes, I really wonder why it's happened," responded
Sukhjit, for once agreeing with his wife.

"Why don't we take him to Bah Rit the nongshat?"
said a by-now very jolly Teibor Dohling, sipping his gin
and tonic.

"Who is that?" asked Indra eagerly.

"Oh! He's one who can see the signs of what may have
caused the ailment and suggest remedies when all else
fails," contributed Giginia smugly.

"Really? How does he go about it?" Sukhjit put down
his glass of beer and leaned towards Teibor.

"Well, let me put it very simply ... one has to go to him,
preferably early in the morning, with some rice which has
been kept under the pillow overnight and some eggs. Once
you have settled down he asks you what your problem is
and after a brief discussion he prepares the dieng shat, a
small wooden plank for the puja. Then he takes an egg,
places it on the dieng shat and prays. When he feels the
prayer has been heard he breaks the egg and reads the

signs. He continues the procedure, breaking the eggs one by one till he is satisfied that his prayers are answered and his patient's problem is solved. The way the shell, yolk and white fall on the plank indicates the answers. On the shattered egg on the dieng shat he puts the grains of rice in different spots to read the interpretation. It's complicated, but when you see it ... in fact, you must see the ritual. It's fascinating."

"What kind of questions does one ask?" Sukhjit was by then highly intrigued, as was Indra as she edged closer to Tiebor.

"You can for example ask why you are afflicted with this ailment and if it can be cured and also what the cure is."

"Why one is afflicted?" Indra Sodhi asked, looking puzzled.

"Yes, like it could be genetic, self-created or ... inflicted by others!" said Giginia.

"By others?"

"Yes, for example, through black magic because of enmity or if someone has done a wrong then it comes back to the wrong-doer this way ... in the form of illness or some other calamity ... Don't look so worried Indra, I'm just citing examples," Giginia Dohling tapped the shoulder of her latest fan and laughed.

The wide-eyed children had moved near the adults by then. Saphira hunched up next to her mother, elbows on her knees as she bit her nails absentmindedly.

"Can I ask if I will do well in my tenth?" asked Dalbir, the youngest Sodhi.

"Yes! And you can tell him to enhance the marks," said Gigi and everyone laughed, not because it was not true but because it was a funny kind of truth.

Everyone laughed except Saphira. She first looked at her pale-faced Nah Duh then she looked into Sukhjit's eyes as she heard him speak, "My problem *is* genetic, the doctors *said* so, I don't need to go to the 'nong shat'," he whispered ... a whisper that sounded like the rustling of a snake in the grass.

Saphira kept looking at Sukhjit's eyes and then, suddenly, in a single flash she knew she was looking at the eyes of her uncle's murderer.

WANBOK
THE STEPFATHER

The day Wanbok was getting a second stepfather he felt so happy and elated when he woke up that, after a while, it rattled him. He quickly slid to the floor, did ten push-ups then got up and opened the window to let the fresh air in. He inhaled slowly and correctly just as the yoga teacher had instructed him, not the way he went through the motions every day just to get it over with. He felt the difference. He felt better. That little knot deep, deep inside had disappeared.

It had rained all night and the grass and leaves and slightly ragged hedges glistened moist green in the summer sun. Wan's mother had wanted to wait till July to get married. Three months was, she thought, a decent period for a romance to be accepted as a precursor to matrimony for a woman of her age. She had met her husband-to-be in February. She talked to Wanbok about it and asked what he thought about the date and month, once she had established the fact that he approved and liked Boris Neinnong. That was important for her.

Actually it had happened suddenly with the refreshing spontaneity one would associate with a teenage boy. One morning before going off to school, as he was gulping down his cornflakes and milk, he told his mother, "Mei, you are lonely and so am I, why don't you marry Uncle Boris?" His mother looked at him and then quickly looked away but did not reply. He knew, however, that she felt good. He certainly did after the outburst. He felt relieved and soothed like when a sudden splash of sunlight lighted up a grey January morning.

So Wanbok's mother had decided on July but the elders advised against it. In July, the month of Naitung, people in these eastern hills did not marry mainly because of the inclement weather just as they avoided April, the month of Iaiong. In April it was the winds, in July the rains. So she gave in to the insistence of her parents and maternal uncles. She felt embarrassed to fuss too much about dates and details; she knew it would only invite unnecessary, unwanted comments and smirks. After all how would they understand that for her it was like the first time, the very first.

She was immensely touched when her Ma Deng, her middle mama, suggested that although there would be no rituals, the groom and his party would be given the traditional welcome and prayers would be said and blessings bestowed. A feast would follow with two pigs and a dozen chickens slaughtered and, of course, there would be the endless tea party with the usual cakes and savouries ordered from Guidetti's. The suggestion was readily accepted by everyone in the room. Wanbok was as happy as his mother because her previous marriage had been just a cut and dried court affair with tea and dinner afterwards. Uncle Toki and his mother danced the night away along with the other guests but it could have been just any party.

It was different now, ever since Boris Neinnong entered their lives. He could see the glow on his mother's face slowly returning during the past few months like a hesitant traveller from faraway. He also sensed her quiet joy and revelled in it.

Labiangmon Swer was very attractive at thirty-six with a voice as smooth as silk and a body svelte and graceful as a swan. She was a caring mother, sensitive to her young son's feelings, never once embarrassing or hurting him. She made sure that her child's life was her top priority; that was an unsaid rule among her clan and all the other clans.

Wanbok closed half the window as the breeze suddenly whipped up into a strong wind, which buffeted and tossed the leaves and blew them into the room. The neighbours and close relatives had already arrived to help. The sound of their cheerful chatter drifted up to Wanbok's room as they sipped steaming cups of tea and munched butter biscuits.

Wanbok was relieved that Trevor, his best friend who had come to spend the night, was fast asleep in the next bed, oblivious. He bolted the window and returned to bed. There was plenty of time; the wedding ceremony was scheduled for 2 p.m. He quietly switched on the TV, automatically punching 8 for the NDTV morning news. This was a good habit instilled by Brother Rosario who made the boys write ten lines daily on what they saw and heard on the programme and what they thought about it. That morning the news focussed on the United States stepping up pressure for Indian troops to be sent to Iraq. Wanbok winced as he watched. He and his friends felt very let down by the US, a country they all looked up to. That the most powerful nation in the world could be so devious just for the sake of oil filled their young minds with new fears and insecurities – it was like having an inept and unreliable head of the family. Fortunately, Wanbok never had to face that. "Stupid Bush," he muttered and switched off the television.

As he peeled his night suit off and readied his bath, he thought of his first stepfather, Tokin Bareh. He was so much like the navy blue and white bathroom he gifted Wan on his tenth birthday, flashy yet elegant, luxurious yet solid, huge yet cozy. Tokin Bareh was a dashing businessman and coal king. He was an absolute joy to be with and Wan loved him dearly. He came in to Wanbok's life when he was four. Pa Tokin taught Wan so many delightful things in those eight glorious years while he was married to Labiangmon – football, cricket, carom, songs by the Beatles and how to master mathematic tables in the quickest possible way. The trips during the winter holidays were magical – Kolkata, the Andamans, Goa, Mumbai, Rajasthan and one unforgettable skiing trip to Kufri on their way to Manali.

Every so often he would remember the snow-covered hillsides shimmering white, so white it hurt the eyes, the black slate rooftops loaded with snow and the pine trees dripping snowflakes that showered from heaven like confetti. He could almost hear the shouts of joy as Pa To, his mother and he played in the winter sun, throwing snowballs at each other on those distant slopes. He could still see the many strollers, both locals and tourists who stopped and stared at them, smiling wistfully at the happy threesome. Wanbok had felt so proud of his beautiful mother and handsome stepfather, so well groomed and tastefully attired in colourful winter wear, exuding health and happiness. That was the last holiday they spent together.

In April that year, three months after the Kulu-Manali trip, Labiangmon was sent to Delhi for a ten week training programme by her office. Wanbok missed his mother but was secure and well looked after in his grandparents' home in Nongthymmai where his aunt, his mother's younger sister and her husband and two children also lived. Tokin Bareh spent those ten weeks in his native Jaintia Hills setting up a factory in his village close to the main highway that snaked languidly down to Assam. Every weekend he would come to Shillong, open up the house and take Wanbok out for the night. They would hit the town together, dining out in the best restaurants and bring back a movie to watch later. He really enjoyed staying up till 1 am. He felt all grown-up and sophisticated.

Yet as the weeks passed by he could not help but notice that Pa To had begun to drink heavily. He would continue to drink after dinner even though he'd already had his usual three drinks before the meal. One night the phone rang just as the movie started. Pa To dragged the phone away to the passage and talked for a long time. When he returned to his seat next to Wan, Wan asked if it was his mother, Pa To simply replied 'No' and looked straight ahead at the television screen. Wanbok's heart stopped for a second but Jackie Chan was far too captivating. Wan had an unusual gift: he could divert his gloomy thoughts by switching channels. This was what kept him happy and always smiling.

Life carried on, and then, just as spring was maturing into summer, his mother returned. Tokin loved and respected Labiangmon too much not to tell her the truth. He had, he confessed, got involved with his manager's young daughter, Merika who was pregnant and threatening suicide if he did not marry her. There was very little that Labiangmon could do. She was left with just one alternative.

Wanbok could not fathom how hurt his mother was but he could sense sadness drifting in and out of the house all day. He was not even sure what had happened but both his mother and Pa To came quietly one day and sat down in his room. After a long stretch of what adults call 'polite conversation' his mother informed him gently "Pa To is going away to Jaintia Hills to work and to live on his own." "I will come and see you as often as I can," Pa To added, his voice just above a whisper. That was when Wan became very close to Trevor because his parents too had separated recently and they could share each other's pain just as they had shared their joys and boyhood secrets.

The day Tokin Bareh finally left, he held Wanbok close to his heart. They both wept as Labiang sat in the corner of the verandah and continued with her knitting and her younger sister sat next to her, head down, chewing kwai. Tokin presented Wanlang with a mobile, "You ring me anytime son, anytime, day or night. Promise. Look after yourself ... and your mother, Wan."

"Don't cry Pa, I know these things happen, that's what they say ... and, of course, I'll call you," Wanbok replied with a smile once his tears and his childhood had seeped away, forever.

He was thirteen and heart-broken. He knew, however, that in the world he lived in, such twists and turns took place. In school they discussed it all the time. It always helped. So many years had passed since that day. Four years to be exact.

* * *

When Wanbok stepped back in to his room after a most invigorating bath he found his friend, Trevor, awake.

Trevor looked pensive and had propped himself up on his left arm, his chin cupped in his hand.

"Hi Trev! Slept well?"

"Hmn, hmn"

"Hmn, hmn? What does that mean?"

"Why are you looking so serious man? Would you like some tea? Horlicks?"

"Later."

"Fine, but cheer up man. Had a bad dream or something?"

"Look, Wan, are you sure you are okay?"

"Of course. We've discussed it all haven't we? You were so positive then, what's the matter now Trev?"

"Look man, I was positive, I said positive things for your sake but it isn't all that easy … "

"Of course, it isn't. I know that Trev, I discovered that the day I grew up, the day Pa To left."

"Yeah … "

"The day Pa To left my Meirad sent for me and I went with Mei and Nahnah. I remember she had laid out quite an elaborate tea, which I ate in a daze. She came straight to the point. You know grannies they always manage to solve it all, just solve it all … "

"What did she say?"

"She said, 'Wan, God makes us go through bad times so that we may grow up. Some grow up and sink, others grow up and rise. You, my grandson, will rise'."

Trevor was quiet for a second and then broke into uncontrollable sobs.

"Trevor, Trev, stop it. What's up Trev?"

"I wish I had a granny … I wish I had, both mine are dead. If I did I wouldn't have had to go through all those years of … of … "

"I know but Brother Rosario got you out of that. God sends someone – always. He was as kind as any granny. He didn't expel you when he caught you stoned, he was so kind … "

"I know, I know but I went through hell before that … "

"Yeah, but now you have risen … above all that crap."
"Wan, you are so brave. Tell me, man, who is your real father?"

"What?"

"Sorry, sorry Wan, SORRY, SORRY, SORRY."

"No, no, I am shocked because … because I've never thought about it."

"Forget it man"

"No Trev, you are right – who is my biological father actually … Pa To was a true father … Pa To was a true father to me, he was so good that I had begun thinking that he was my father … He came into my life when I was, I think, four, so I've never been curious …"

"Yeah, I guess … "

"But, I think, I should find out now, I'll ask Pa To, he is my best friend, my best grown-up friend. He'll tell me."

* * *

Labiangmon sat at her dressing table brushing her long, lustrous hair. On two mulas on either side of her sat her cousins Gigi and Odette.

"Come on Labiang say something … " Gigi entreated her eyes bright with excitement.

"Something."

"Come on La, don't be mean, I haven't taken leave and come all the way from Mumbai to attend this great occasion to hear silly jokes. You can't do this to me. Come on, we have to dance, sing, laugh but first tell me. Tell me how it all happened. This is just too romantic!"

"Odette, I am not sixteen … and … "

"It's … it's not the first time. Ok fine … but you are glowing, you look sixteen. Oh! La I am so happy for you. Tell me … "

"Odette, please … you tell Gigi … "

"It's your story, La, you tell … "

* * *

In everyone's life certain things happen that are predestined and unpreventable. Strangely for Labiang this happened on the very first day of the New Year. It was like a true beginning.

She was on her way to her friend's place for New Year lunch. She was stuck in a traffic jam in Tirot Sing Road when, at the Khyndai Lad crossing, a car purred up next to her. Only people who had no road etiquette would double wait in a jam on a narrow road and Labiang was irritated. Everyone waited, single file, except for that one car. Labiang didn't look around to see who it was. As usual she continued to road dream. She could sense the intense, continuous stare of the driver of the errant car and wondered what kind of bumpkin he must be but she did not give in. She continued to look ahead. After some time all the cars began to move ahead. She looked around her automatically to check if her car was aligned in the queue. It was then that she saw him. He who had been watching her all that while smiling, a smile that took her back to a distant past. The lips were tired and blackened with age and cigarette smoke and the hair had thinned and peppered but Labiang recognized him.

In February when the elections were held she saw him again. And again on television and in the papers and one day, she found herself listening to him speak at a rally at the Fire Brigade Ground on the Nongthymnai highway. "I request you all to always give your best to your country, your community, your family and yourself. John F. Kennedy once said, 'Ask not what your country can do for you. Ask what you can do for your country.'" The crowd cheered. An elderly man next to Labiang asked his companion, "What did he say? Do you know English?" His companion answered, "No, but this man has something about him, he's no ordinary man. I will give him my vote definitely." Labiang felt a lump in her throat as her heart swelled with pride much against her will. "No, no ... don't let this happen," she shouted soundlessly, deep inside, as tears coursed down her windswept cheeks.

In March when the results were announced and he was victorious he threw a big party not in his official residence but at his mother's house in the same locality where Labiang lived. She had hesitated about going but her cousins kept on and on telling her, "Come on Labiang forget the past, live for the present." So she went. He was wearing his favourite attire – casual trousers in beige, a brown checked shirt and a dark tan suede jacket. An old muffler, a little faded with age but well preserved hung casually from his neck. A wave of tenderness filled her whole being and she bit her lip to stem the flow of long forgotten emotions that threatened to overwhelm her. When he rang up that night and proposed she was prepared but she just kept quiet … as she always did. That was why it took so long.

"That's what happened," Labiang whispered stroking the dhara she was going to wear – an appropriate purple with a silver border. She always had a preference for white and had girlhood dreams of getting married in the traditional white and gold with white orchids in her hair. Most dreams don't come true, however, and this was one of them. White was allowed only for the virgins; even among non-Christians. So she had tucked away the dream in an unfrequented corner of her heart, long ago.

* * *

Wanbok dialled Tokin Bareh's mobile.

"Pa?"

"Wan! Wan how are you? I am so glad you called. I wanted to talk to you when I heard the good news."

"Yes, I am happy for Mei … ."

"I am happy for you too, Wan. Boris Neinnong is a very good man … "

"Like you Pa, I hope he's like you, I remember all the good times … "

"Wan you are a gem … Thank you … Life is full of surprises. I had to move on see?"

"Pa?"

"Yes?"

"Pa, tell me who is my biological father?"

"What?"

"Who is … "

"You mean your mother hasn't told you?"

"No, she's never told me because I'd never asked … I'd never thought about it till today."

"Wan, today is the greatest homecoming for your mother and father. Eventually everyone returns to where they truly belong."

"What are you saying Pa To?"

"Wan, I feel privileged to be the one to tell you that Boris Neinnong is your biological father. Your mother and Boris were in love since they were in school but both families disapproved because an earlier marriage alliance between the two families had ended in tragedy. The resentment was so severe that even when the elders knew you were on the way, they still put their foot down about the marriage. Time heals and … "

"Pa, you mean I'm a … bastard?"

"Wan in our community every child is born legitimate – it is his birthright except in certain forbidden unions. Boris is not your mother's clansman. He's not related in any way. This union is completely legal and accepted. Boris is a good man, a great man and he is your father. Congratulations, son, sorry Wan … "

"No, Pa To, son."

"Congratulations son … I wish you all happiness and God bless you."

ERIKLANG
ONE RAINY NIGHT[*]

The woman watched the rain lashing against the window with a certain aggression which always unsettled her. She poured herself another glass of Sohiong wine and wished she had not refused her friend Laphisha's invitation to dinner. She sipped the wine and let her eyes wander away to the opposite hillock where the lights of the houses shone like glow worms. An enchanting sight it was, reminiscent of her childhood days in Simla, now called Shimla.

How she loved Shimla where her father, a Central Services officer, was posted in the Department of Post and Telegraph. When he got a posting back to Shillong she missed the place deeply, the sights, the sounds and smells all inextricably linked to their maid and her little daughter, Runa. She was so young, only six, and could not even express her pain. It used to hurt her like a fresh wound and for months she would get up in the middle of the night crying, sucking her thumb. She felt that same kind

* First published in *Celebrating 50 years of Indian Literature*, Sahitya Akademi, 2004

of hurt that evening and wondered why. Maybe because
Eriklang, her son, had promised to be home early and
he wasn't. She missed him, her naughty, wayward child.
How much she had looked forward to this Saturday so
she could be with him, cook his favourite dishes and chat.
How often did she see him during the week after all? She
was always so busy with the work in the office and he with
college. She wondered why he didn't keep his promise to
return home early. She felt an empty fear in the pit of her
stomach. It was almost second nature to her ever since
her husband passed away soon after her mother's demise.
Two pillars of her home had crashed down one after the
other; it was tough.

Outside the rain had suddenly stopped, so typical of
Shillong weather. Only the wind was left to continue its
nocturnal concert. The sound of millions of crickets in the
hedges pierced through the quiet. She got up quickly from
her chair and put on her favourite Yanni tape. On the soft
carpet she perfected a waltz with a glass of warm wine in
one hand and emptiness in the other.

* * *

Earlier she used to miss her young husband, Arlang
terribly.

Cancer had claimed him three years ago, leaving behind
a huge void which she found difficult to fill. While her
husband was struggling with his illness, she had tried her
best to nip her daughter Klarisa's romance in the bud.
Her beau was a doctor in England, a Khasi all right and
he belonged to the same church but he lived thousands of
miles away. She failed miserably. Three months before her

husband expired, Klarisa got married to Paul Khongwir and went away. Arlang was, of course, ecstatic about the match and in spite of his illness looked happy and handsome at the wedding. He always admired professionals and the thought of his daughter living in postcard perfect England cheered him. In that she found great comfort. Yet, after a while, with Arlang gone away forever and Eric away in school, life became unbearably lonely and that was when she made a decision that nobody with her means and education would do: Eriklang would join college in Shillong. Erik seemed happy in the beginning and she was relieved and grateful. The happy interlude, however, did not last long.

A few months after he joined college he stopped communicating with his friends who were in school with him in Darjeeling. They would phone him and bombard him with e-mails and the girls with cards but he sent no reply. She tried so hard to encourage Erik to keep in touch but he was resolute in his decision to keep them out of his life. Along with that came the late nights and the occasional night out. She had thrown three parties for him and done her utmost to make his new friends comfortable. She found them a little scruffy but that didn't prevent her from taking out her best glasses and crockery and preparing a sumptuous spread on his last birthday. The following morning she got up at dawn before her daily help arrived to empty the ash trays, wash the glasses, throw away the cartons of Real Juice and hide the empty bottles.

As the room settled back into shape it suddenly struck her that Erik's three non–tribal friends, Sujoy Mitra, Bobby Singh and Rithik Goswami had stopped telephoning and, at the party, were conspicuous by their absence. She

searched for them because she was fond of them but they
were nowhere in sight. She stood rooted in the middle of
the room hugging a misplaced cushion and decided that
she would talk to Erik and find out from him the following
morning. But when the time came she forgot.

She felt sheepish clearing up the remains of the party but
she certainly didn't want Bini the maid to spread stories
about Erik and his lenient mother because of two bottle of
Smirnoff and ash trays overflowing with stubs. She didn't
think she was lenient, leave alone over-indulgent. Her son
was a college going nineteen year old.

When Erik turned eleven he was packed off to a
boarding school in Darjeeling. Arlang, sensitive and
intelligent, also knew it would do her a world of good to
travel and let Erik be on his own. She cried all the way
there, secretly of course, while Arlang and Anjali diverted
and entertained Erik on the drive down to Guwahati, in
the plane to Bagdogra and the picturesque drive up to the
hill-station.

Erik settled in very well. He became the school Games
Captain in his last year and topped the class in Geography
and Botany. He would get admission into a college in
Delhi quite easily. The two months after his result was
declared were terrible. She was compelled to make a very
selfish decision. It felt strange like being draped in an alien
costume that revealed all the wrong parts of her body.
But she was lonely and insecure and wanted desperately
for at least one family member to be with her. Again and
again she tried to explain her motives to herself and get
some comfort.

* * *

Outside the wind kept moaning around the house and rustling the leaves in the trees. Why wasn't Erik home? She flung the question at the wind that moaned and sighed in the trees and got no answer. For nature there are no questions and no answers. Everything just is, complete in itself, from the beginning of time.

* * *

Erik woke up late that morning. He sat sipping his tea with eyes closed, letting the sun soak in. Then she watched him go upstairs back to his room to wash and change. She waited outside wearing her sweetest smile and asked him where he was going since it was Saturday and college was closed. He stopped when he heard her question and turned towards her, eyes narrowing and uttered just one word "Why?" She was so startled by the response that she offered no answer but simply sat on the garden bench under the chestnut tree, her eyes smarting. She looked up at the sky. The colour reminded her of a single scene in a village near Kalimpong: a little, black-roofed cottage by the roadside fronted by rows and rows of cornflowers, still and poised in the morning light. She couldn't stop there as she had wished because there were too many people in the car. The scene was, however, imprinted indelibly in her mind. She relived the memory and gained some strength as she watched her son driving off in the Maruti, without once looking back.

Confused and desolate she found herself walking up to his room. She inhaled the fragrance of the after-shave that still lingered in the air and opened the window. It was a west-facing room so the noon sun had just arrived, streaming in strong and bright. She made his bed stroking the sheets and the pillows, taking her time, and laying the quilt gently on it as if Erik were lying there, a child still. As she lifted the bedcover from the chair a sweater fell out and slid down to the floor. She picked it up and dusted it several times in front of the window then she buried her face in it to ascertain from the smell if it was ready for a wash. It was a habit of hers that always used to make Arlang laugh. She smiled as she folded the sweater, deciding to put it back.

The chest of drawers of polished dark wood and brass knobs was a wedding gift from her grandmother. Her mother had bought it from an English family who left Shillong to return to England during the Second World War. She leaned forward to open the last drawer. Woollens and shawls were always kept in the last drawer for some reason. Much to her surprise she found she couldn't open it. She put the sweater on the chair, sat down on the carpet and pulled hard, as hard as she could but the drawer wouldn't open. It wasn't stubborn, it wasn't jammed, it was quite simply locked. The drawer never had a key although provision was always there for a locking system. Why did Erik get it done and when?

* * *

Outside, the wind had ceased and she opened the window and breathed in the exhilarating aroma of wet earth after a shower. She kept on inhaling, releasing the tension within her with every breath. For a long time she just stared and stared at the star-spangled sky, inky black like the sequinned gown she once wore at a ball in a Calcutta club. It was after that magical wine soaked night that Erik was conceived, in a suite at the Kenilworth, her favourite hotel.

It was almost ten. Erik was nowhere in sight, not even a phone call. Where was he? Why was he so curt in the morning? Why, why was that one drawer locked? She popped some pine nuts, sent by Klarisa, into her mouth and munching noisily, she climbed upstairs to her son's room.

Of course she felt funny. She felt she was prying. She felt ashamed and bit her lower lip, as her legs kept ascending the wooden staircase, steadily. The room was dark and she groped for the switch which the electrician had placed in an inconvenient corner, too close to the inbuilt cupboard. Light flooded the room spreading on the Fabindia bedcover of grey and blue and climbing up the walls coloured with posters of Bon Jovi, Mariah Carey and a startling black and white sketch of the enigmatic Che Guevera.

She yanked at the drawer once, twice but it resisted her valiant efforts. She sat on the carpet and felt a sudden shooting pain in her stomach. She doubled up and sobbed, missing her husband terribly. In her mind she cried out, "Ar, Ar please help me. What is happening, Arlang?" She knew there was something seriously wrong. Surely the drawer did not contain just drinks and drugs and pornographic delights expected of wayward teenagers. Erik was definitely not an alcoholic and too healthy and pink-checked to be on drugs.

There was one drawer that she hadn't touched that morning, the top most. It was so tidy and clean, the shirts and tee shirts folded and so neatly layered that she left it as it was. She had only settled the second drawer where sweaters and pullovers had been shoved in haphazardly, barely making enough space for the one she found on the chair outside.

The top drawer opened very easily. She stared at the contents and winced. In the morning, in the hurry, she didn't notice the old shirts and tee shirts of Erik's school days kept separately in a pile on the left. The casual ones were in the middle heap and the very stylish designer collection piled on the right. She looked at them lying innocently like slumbering babes and wondered what on earth she was doing there. Yet the sight of the grey and dark blue sweat shirt with 'Games Captain' emblazoned on the front wrenched her heart and her eyes misted. She stretched her hand and bending down a little she pulled it out. Some thing small and shiny clattered to the ground. It was a key.

It was difficult to open the drawer because of the damp. Finally it slid open at a slant, like someone looking askance. She kept on pushing and pulling at it until she managed to open it completely. Her heart was thumping and her head began to spin. The drawer gaped open to reveal its deadly contents: an AK 47 lying languidly like a sleeping reptile amidst cartridges and Chinese-made smaller weapons. She gasped and recoiled with horror.

Scenes flashed across her mind in quick succession. Each scene confirmed forever that those late nights and nights out and Erik's withdrawal and distancing himself from her and his old friends were not, as she had thought, innocent and natural. One memory which she had flung far far away into the furthest recesses of her mind came back, rising from the depths ... one autumn night when she was about to fall asleep after watching a late night movie she heard Erik returning from his friend's house. She was very relieved because there was a curfew on. She remembered it was autumn because she had started using her quilt and what she heard next made her sit up. The water in Erik's bathroom was running. He was bathing and also washing some clothes. It was 1a.m. and no one bathed in Shillong at 1a.m.

In the morning when the maid came to wash and clean, Erik was still fast asleep. She instructed the maid to start with the washing and she tiptoed into her son's room. In a bucket she found the clothes he had worn the previous day – a pair of blue jeans, a long-sleeved blue and white check shirt, white cotton socks and underwear – washed and rinsed. She took the bucket out and decided that she would rinse the clothes once more and then hang them out herself, "I am being a good mummy," she sang to herself as if there was nothing to worry about and all was well with the world. She continued to hum quietly as she went about her chores. She continued to hum until it was time to peg the shirt on the clothesline – as she held it against the sun small splotches of yellow stains were visible. She knew that just as curry stains turned red, blood stains turned yellow. With hands cold and trembling she shoved the shirt into an old plastic bag and hid it behind her shoe rack, "He has hurt himself somewhere but I won't wake him up till I get back from office," she told herself firmly, taking deep breaths to steady her nerves and that was exactly what she did.

There is one thing about offices—they take you away to a different world where domestic and other personal problems are totally submerged under hundreds of files, steaming cups of tea and the incessant, mindless chatter. That was exactly what happened and by the time she got home the memory of the previous night seemed distant as though it had never happened. Erik was watching a one-day international cricket match with his friends. There was so much laughter and glee in the air. She dug out the packet from under the shoe rack and flung it into the rubbish pit at the edge of the garden, below the old oak tree. Then she changed into a caftan and sank into her favourite chair reminiscing about a row of cornflowers dancing in the northern light, faraway, long ago.

She remembered it all.

* * *

"Why my son, why?" she whispered, her eyes roaming all over the room resting on every single object of her child's. "Do you understand what this is all about, do you believe in all this ... or is it just because you want to be accepted? Oh God! Erik, my child you have always had this problem. Erik have I failed you somehow, somewhere ... please come back soon my child and at least tell me ... all you have to do is tell me ... We'll ... We'll work it out ... we'll ... "

Just then the phone rang. She picked up the extension upstairs, next to Erik's room.

"Good evening, Madam, we are very sorry to inform you ... err ... I am speaking from the police station ... some accomplices of militants have been..."

The phone dropped from her hand and dangled like a severed head, jerking piteously. Devastated, she collapsed on the floor and wept because she knew she would never get her answers.

The rain began to pour down again in sheets of dense gray. Along with it the wind returned and both these gentle giants of nature held this house of sorrow in their arms.

RIIAKA
THE GIRL IN A BLUE JAINSEM[*]

In March the winds blow hard in these hills, crisp and cold, defying the early-spring sun. Riiaka, eyes half shut, clutched her sheaf of papers and her handbag tightly and braved the wind with determined steps as her jainsem flapped on her lithe body, like a bird in panic.

It was one of those days. She had left her registers at home and had to write her class notes on borrowed paper. In her great hurry to leave for college, for she had overslept, she couldn't find tights to wear beneath her dress to match her jainsem and protect her from the cold. Riiaka enjoyed wearing trousers and salwar kameezes but not so long ago the locality boys had sent threatening messages to all the college-going girls to avoid wearing 'foreign clothes' or else! Riiaka wasn't quite sure about the status of trousers so a few still hung in her cupboard. The salwar suits were

---

* First published by Samyukta, *Woman's Initiatives*, Kerala, vol. III, 2003.

tucked away deep inside a huge trunk under some old curtains.

Riiaka had passed the Main Post Office and the banks and was about to reach the photo studio opposite the old Presbyterian Church, when the wind suddenly wrenched her papers from her hands and scattered them on the ground. As she watched them floating down in mad ballet swirls her jainsem lifted up to her armpits and blinded her. She closed her eyes tight, steadying her legs and her nerves, shaken, embarrassed as she tried to control the dress beneath her jainsem that had also ballooned out imperiously with the last sweep of the wind. Her nails dug desperately into her bag as she tried to protect the money for her weekend shopping on the way home: some pork and vegetables for the family and fruit for herself. The season of oranges was over and her mother and grandmother had stopped eating fruits. They would now wait for the plums and pears to come. Riiaka was different. She could not do without fruit. So she would buy some papaya and grapes and pomegranate from the Bengali fruit vendor in Police Bazaar. "She's different," her grandmother would mutter as her lips would gently part into an enigmatic smile. Her mother would nod and keep the fruit in a bowl made in China, rimmed with red hibiscus.

Riiaka could feel the human traffic sail past her, defying the wind. She pulled her jainsem down impatiently, confused, angry, as her bag thudded to the pavement. As she bent down to retrieve it, another pair of hands, brown and strong reached there first. She watched them lift up her bag and in the process noticed the black Bally's that shone like a mirror, the grey flannel trousers, the navy blue blazer, the amused light brown eyes and tousled hair and then a voice. The voice seemed to have travelled from a long distance and held the warmth of honey and wood smoke, the fragrance of musk and cigars.

"Here you are ... your papers, all of them, relax, relax. Some have got a little dirty but ... "

"Thank you, thank you, it's okay, my goodness, really nice of you, thanks ... bye."

"You're frozen. Come let's have a cup of tea somewhere."

"What? No, no, please. I had tea in college before I left – cups and cups of tea and singharas and lalmohans. Thank you, bye, bye."

"Oh! ok. Your jainsem is so beautiful. I love blue, it's my favourite colour."

Riiaka fled. She raced down the pavement without looking back. She didn't stop till she had crossed over into Police Bazaar and mingled with the sea of people. She walked quickly clutching her bag, her papers and her fear close to her heart. What if some of the boys from her locality had seen her talking to a 'dkhar', a plainsman, an outsider? What explanation would she give? If they wanted to harass her they would pretend they didn't believe her. That's all. There was no one to protect her – no father, no mama, no brother. Her father "went away" her grandmother explained to her, "back to Punjab. His family opposed his alliance with your mother." Her brother, Aibok had walked out of the house after a massive argument with her mother. Riiaka's stomach churned and tears welled up at the memory. "Mei was wrong, so wrong, so wrong. Why didn't I speak out? How could she, how could she refuse to hock part of the property for the loan Bah wanted? Starting a car-care centre was his dream. He is a boy – so what, so what, Mei, so what? He, too, is your child. What tradition? In a world where money is so important, where nothing else is as important – things have to change, Mei. How could you?" She was leaning against a pillar near Dreamland Cinema, tears trickling down her face. The kind-faced Marwari who owned the shop took out a clean handkerchief and gave it to her. "It's the wind, hep, it's the wind. Oh dear! So much grit has got into your eyes. Good for you, hep, if it all comes out." Riiaka smiled weakly and thanked him. She walked down the dark, dank steps slowly, counting each one, to divert the pain inside.

Captain Vinod Sarin walked down Ward's Lake and watched the water lilies changing colour in the fading light. He walked slowly, trying to sort out his scattered thoughts but the wind kept whipping him, shattering his thoughts into smithereens. He crossed the wooden bridge that spanned the waters like a hunchback and climbed up the slope. He could see the lights of the hotel and sighed with relief at the welcoming sight of some shelter from the onslaught of the March wind. The little bar in Pinewood Hotel was empty but warm and cozy as he sipped a glass of brandy. He avoided the club. He would have met too many people he knew. He did not want the recent experience to dissipate with watered down drinks and predictable small talk.

As the cognac slowly and languidly warmed his throat, his thoughts began to settle down. Vinod smiled and closed his eyes and let his mind travel back to the moments that had just passed. He saw, all over again, the perfect body sailing with the wind, blue, sky-blue jainsem flapping on it like seagull wings, the little heart-shaped face, dark brown eyes – so much like his – and lips that pouted vulnerability and warmth. He loved the way the girl got nervous and rattled off the goodies she had devoured for tea at her college canteen. The way she referred to samosas as singharas and gulabjamuns as lalmohans. He found it so charming, so Northeastern. His heart pounded as he took out a piece of paper from his wallet and quickly scribbled what he could remember was written on one of the books. Name-Riiaka, College – St. Mary's, Class – 2nd yr. Political Science, Address – Hazelmere Cottage, Jaiaw. There was something else after Jaiaw. He searched his memory desperately but to no avail. He summoned the young Khasi waiter. "I am not Khasi, Sir, I am Garo. Wait, I'll call Cyril, he's Khasi." Cyril solved his problem after much juggling with words beginning with L. It was Langsning, Jaiaw Langsning. Vinod had had a tough time memorizing the girl's address as he gathered the dancing papers from the footpath. In fact, he was amazed that he had managed to do it.

It was tough but worth it for, at last, Vinod was sure of one till-then uncertainty: who he wanted to marry. It felt a little crazy He, however, had always been accused of being an incorrigible romantic, a doomed creature by his aunts who looked after him after his mother's demise and whose conversation lately was always punctuated by two words – 'suitable' and 'correct'. He was their brother's only child. Vinod, handsome, well to do, a major in the Army, an eligible bachelor, was getting posted to the Northeast. A tacit state of emergency was declared: a bride must be found at the earliest.

He winced, took a big gulp of brandy and then couldn't stop smiling thinking of his aunts clucking over glasses of nimbu pani in their hot dusty farms in the plains of Punjab,

planning his marriage. He realized, of course that all he
knew of the girl he'd bumped into on the windswept road
was what she had for tea and the most basic information
written on her book. A bit embarrassed, he looked around
the room in case someone had managed to decode the smile
playing on his lips and the thoughts that raced through his
mind. Tonight he would ring up his father in Jalandhar and
tell him to stop looking around for prospective 'bahus'.
His eldest aunt, Mala Buaji, especially should be firmly
informed of his decision. He smiled at the thought and the
memory of an exquisite girl in a blue jainsem.

Riiaka opened the white wrought iron gate and waded
through the heap of fallen leaves speckled white with pear
blossoms that the wind had brought down. She rang the
bell and stumbled in right into her grandmother's ample
bosom.

"Sorry, sorry Meirad, sorry … "

"It's all right, it's all right – but why are you so pale
darling? Iris, ko Iris, make Ri some tea, her hands are
frozen. So what if you didn't get the pork darling. I'll
make some vegetable stew with shrimps instead. The shad
is almost here and you must dance baieit. Next year is far
away and maybe, maybe … you'll no longer be able to
dance no darling?"

Her grandmother gathered Riiaka in her arms and
chuckled happily in anticipation of a possible wedding
in the house.

Only virgins participate in the after-harvest thanksgiving
dance held annually during April and May. Riiaka and her
brother danced every year except once when the family
was still mourning the death of her only 'mama', her uncle.
They also danced in neighbouring villages and in their

native town, near the Bangladesh border. Virgin girls and boys and men of all ages, gorgeously arrayed in silks, velvets, brocades and ornaments of gold, silver and coral move reverently to the music of the traditional pipes and drums. The Shad Suk Mynsiem, the Dance of Peaceful Hearts is the only form of community worship among the Khasis, those who are not converted into other faiths and who worship God, U Blei, Omnipresent, Omnipotent, Omniscient, Imageless and Formless.

"Of course, I'll dance, Meirad. Of course, I will. I only wish Bah was also here."

"Quiet Ri, don't, don't mention your brother's name in this house. He left us didn't he? He defied us and got married to that girl and left."

"Meirad, that's not true, you know it's not true. You and Mei refused to help him … his wife is a lovely woman. I really like Pauline, I do. And how could you deprive him of the little sum he asked for – how could you?"

"Quiet, quiet. I know she even converted your brother. As for what your brother asked for – well if he had not married so inappropriately … I would have given him something. We have to change with the times. Some families already have. I know money is important, you told me that before, but it doesn't solve all problems. There is no one single remedy for problems. Oh Ri, my love, actually in life there are no such things as problems. Experiences which don't suit us and which we don't like, we call problems. Oh! I know what you are going to say next. Yes, you can't avoid problems or swat them like unwanted flies. You have to face them like you would an intruder. Have your tea and rest a bit. This weather has unsettled you. Iris ko Iris make some tea for Ri. Problems are the rapids in the flow of life, they are part of life. Let's forget them for a while. The wind has unsettled us. Go darling, have some tea."

Riiaka swallowed her words and her tears and did as she was told. She had had a long discussion with her cousin, Saralin who was a junior lawyer. Traditional laws were different she had said, and only girls inherited. The elders of each family, however, especially the maternal uncles, could decide how much the sons of the family should inherit. Her only mama was no more. She would start attending the clan meetings Riiaka decided, she could then consult the elders of her clan. That was the other alternative, the only one.

She wanted to pray and, for once felt the need for photographs and idols like the ones in the homes of her friends but in the end, her upbringing prevailed and she simply sat down, closed her eyes and tried to pray. One does not have to look at the sun to feel its warmth, one does not have to see a bird to hear its song, one does not have to touch Truth to know what's right. God is everywhere, in everything and in everyone. That was what she was taught. She knew it all but, that day, she couldn't think straight. Whenever she closed her eyes, a pair of light brown eyes stared back at her. She gave up, stormed into the bathroom and splashed her face with cold water. She went on and on till the deep blush that coloured her cheeks had paled to unremembering.

She sipped her tea. Suddenly her teeth chattered and her hands shook, spilling brown stains on her blue jainsem. Supposing some locality boys had seen her talking to the dkhar. Dkhar. She could smell the strong aroma of wood smoke and honey and musk and cigars; fragrances so strange yet familiar, so distant, yet so close. She had never felt so wonderful before, so special and so completely mesmerized. Riiaka now had something she could only share with herself. She hugged herself and looked around the room in case a prowler had read her secret thoughts.

* * *

His father had said he needed time to think. In fact, he said Vinod should think even harder. It was his life and the whole episode – for God's sake – sounded so unreal and the huge decision based on it, so immature, so impractical. Vinod kept quiet right through the tirade. Deep inside him he was relieved that his father didn't, as feared, scream his lungs out and write to the Commandant. His father sounded calm, in spite of the reprimand.

After a week Brigadier Vivek Kumar Sarin rang up his son to ask if better sense had prevailed. Vinod replied in the affirmative. He was even more sure of his decision. He had been watching the girl going in and out of college, followed her to her house in a borrowed scooter – but didn't go in – and had spoken with her twice over the phone. She shared the same interests as Vinod – reading and music, cooking and gardening, the outdoors and yoga. Yes, she loved salwar kameez and tandoori chicken. She knew where Jalandhar and Dalhousie were and could even spell them, he added light-heartedly. She told him her name meant, You look after her. And when he asked her who was 'you'. She had replied "God of course – who else?" She had laughed. He loved her laugh. He wanted to get to know her better and for that his father must come to Shillong, reconnect with his old army buddies settled in the town and arrange a decent meeting. Vinod certainly did not want to be beaten up by the local boys who would obviously presume he was just out for a good time.

His father's response was silence. A long silence that refused to break even after Vinod kept shouting, "Daddy can you hear me? I love you. Take care." Finally, worried and angry he emailed his father: "Daddy, you are so dry, so unromantic. Your life is one straight line. How would you know what true love is? True love happens like this. Yours was an arranged marriage but, Ma, she was an artist, she would have understood. I wish she was here. She would have explained it all to you. All the same I love you Dad. Try to understand my plight!"

Riiaka watched her mother and grandmother leave Hazelmere Cottage to go and visit a sick relative in the Civil Hospital. She saw them catch a cab on the road below. Once they were out of sight Riiaka bolted her bedroom door and put on the heater. Then she removed the cover from the trunk, unlocked it and creaked the lid open. Out came eight, nine curtains. Quickly she flung them to the floor, her hands shaking. Riiaka looked carefully around her room checking each window, her eyes darting, in case the blinds weren't properly and completely drawn. Satisfied that they were and no one could possibly peep in, she took out a pale pink and lilac salwar kameez suit from the trunk. She spread it out on the bed and stroked it gently, straightening it. Then she removed her jainkyrshah and the dress and did a little pirouette towards the dressing table. Brushing her hair vigorously till it shone she coiled it into a French knot at the nape of her neck. A newly bought Lakme kaajal darkened her eyes and made them even brighter and larger. She used a pale pink lipstick to match the suit. Then, soundlessly, holding her breath, she stepped into the salwar and knotted it and let the kameez slide down her body to her knees before she zipped it up. The dupatta she flung around her like a long scarf. The pink flecked with gold lit up her face, a face that glowed like the autumn sky.

Riiaka lifted the dupatta and moved it around letting the colours play in the light. Yes, lilac was closest to blue since she didn't have a blue suit. From a little oval-shaped mother of pearl box, bought at the college fete, she took out a bindi. As she looked at the mirror she saw nothing else but a little blue circle dotting her forehead. Her eyes had filled up and her whole being was enveloped in the aroma of wood smoke and honey, musk and cigars.

Captain Vinod Sarin opened his mail not a week but nine days after he spoke with his father. Brigadier Sarin sounded very happy and buoyant and sent his best wishes and promised to visit in May or June when the northern plains are at their hottest. He would certainly meet the girl and "let's see, son, let's take it from there." After giving his son more news of his hometown, he ended the letter with a long paragraph, "Vinod you called me dry and unromantic. You are wrong my son. I, too, got hit by a whirlwind once and that too in Shillong! She was a beautiful Khasi widow who was working as a stenographer in the office. Your mother had left with you, as you had to join Prep School. It was crazy of me and I felt terrible for the lady and felt even worse when I had to tell your mother. Vinod, a girl was born out of that union, that dream- like summer infatuation or whatever you choose to call it. Vinod, I would like, if it's all right by you, to meet her and her mother when I come in the summer to help you out with your romance. I don't remember the exact address but she,

too, lived somewhere in Jaiaw. Try to find out. The name
of the house was Hazelmere Cottage; the lady's name was
Iris. Love, Daddy."

KHLAINBOR
THE FINAL DECISION

The day Khlainbor Sing shot his wife and sister began like any other day. Nothing unusual really, a typical April morning filled with buoyant sunshine and the feel of summer in the air. It was certainly not the sort of day that one would associate with such a horrific tragedy, a tragedy of such magnitude, hitherto unheard of in these hills.

When Khlainbor woke up it was half past ten and the sun poured in through the cracks between the wooden planks of his two room shack. It was quiet inside, so quiet he could hear his own heartbeat and the persistent throbbing inside his head. Next to the bed his wife had kept a glass of sohkwit juice. He stirred in two big spoons of sugar and gulped it thirstily. He did that every day. When he felt better he stepped outside to wash, splashing cold water liberally all over his face. Cool, refreshing water that spurted out naturally from the hillside behind his house, from his very own shyngiar. That exhilarating morning ritual always made him feel like a king.

The plot of land had belonged to his mother and, later, after her death, it was inherited by his three sisters. They, in turn, gifted part of it to him when he married Sinora, the most beautiful girl in the village and a friend of his younger sister, Joyla. As Khlainbor dried his face and ruffled his short, unruly mop to chase his headache away, he watched the mauve tresses of the jacaranda floating down with the breeze. He did that every morning, admiring this foreign tree which his brother-in-law, a truck driver had brought all the way from Shillong. After that he made himself a cup of tea.

As he sipped, the warm liquid travelling down his throat to his stomach and then to the rest of his body, flooded him with a sense of well-being and contentment. He always enjoyed this warmth within, complementing the enveloping sunshine that touched his body like a loving parent. He thought of his wife already at work, carrying sand from the river up to the road above for the trucks to carry to the construction site. He, too, would soon go down when his friend Rishod would come to pick him up. This was also routine for Khlain. It happened every day except on those occasional 'dry' days when they had not drunk the night before and they would be up early, along with their wives, at the break of dawn. Khlain felt that familiar pang of guilt sneaking in but he quickly shooed it away like an unwanted fly. "At least, I never abuse and beat my wife, my lovely Sinora. So what if she goes to work an hour earlier than me!" he thought as he lit his pipe. It really was like any other day.

Then Rishod arrived, neither late nor early, but as usual a little after noon, but that day he was not alone. Sanbor, his cousin from the neighbouring village was with him.

It startled Khlainbor a bit because Sanbor had a general store in his village and he seldom deserted it except on Sundays and special holidays. After the usual greetings and exchange of pleasantries, Khlain sat them down and offered them some kwai and red tea. Half-way through the ritual, Rishod pulled his mula close to Khlain and related Sanbor's proposal. It did not take very long. Rishod always articulate and confident, rattled off the plan like an experienced professor.

Khlainbor spilt his tea, apologized, relit his pipe and almost burnt his hand. He tried to speak but couldn't as his heart thumped as if it was about to burst. Two lakhs for so little work! "Sinora, excellent cook that she is, will be able to have the jadoh shop she has always wanted, she has always dreamt about. I will help her and the two of us will make the most perfect pusyep and putharo this side of Nongstoin."

These words raced through his head and danced in his heart as he shook Sanbor's hand and agreed to meet him later in the evening to seal the deal.

As soon as they left Khlain went inside and, humming a favourite ditty, danced around the room hugging his wedding photograph, framed in shiny plastic, close to his heart. Then bolting the door he ran down the hill, crossed the road and stood on a promontory that overlooked the river-bed below. He took a deep breath to contain his excitement as he watched his wife and sister with a group of friends trudging up the hill with bags of sand in their khohs. As they came close to him he stood behind a rock half-hidden and called out to them conspiratorially in a half-whisper and a little wave, like a school boy up to mischief.

"Hep Joyla, your brother has finally made it! Don't ask me how but I have finally made it ... and my dearest Sinora, you are finally going to get your jadoh shop," he gushed, as the women gaped at him, their eyes lighting up like little lamps.

His eyes misted and he felt embarrassed and quickly walked away. When he reached the road he looked back and waved. Joyla and Sinora had removed their khohs from their bodies and were leaning against a rock chatting and laughing. He called out to them and waved and they waved back, their hands fluttering like wang leaves. Khlain had never seen them wave like that before. He felt a lump in his throat and mustering all his courage he blew them a first-time-ever flying kiss. Then without looking back he boarded a passing bus that would take him down to the market-place.

Once there he headed for the largest tea shop which had music and television, where he would, sometimes on rainy afternoons, watch Juhi Chawla films and drool and dream. He ordered a cup of tea with milk and sugar and a plate of rice with chicken curry, something different, not the usual pork and beef dishes –village fare! He suddenly felt as if he hadn't eaten in years. He ate very slowly savouring each mouthful, gazing at the landscape steeped in the late afternoon glow.

Invigorated, Khlainbor paid the woman fifteen rupees with a flourish and did not wait for the change.

He decided to walk the four kilometers across the dappled fields and babbling brooks to meet his new employer. Sanbor had so meticulously chalked out the plan that nothing could go wrong. All Khlain had to do together with his loyal friends was to see that no one hindered the operation. That night he would be paid fifty thousand rupees as advance and after the work was done another one lakh fifty thousand rupees. He shook his head to make sure that he wasn't dreaming.

Aibor, Pynsuk, Madonlang and, of course, Earl and Duke (the handsome twins, brothers of Streamlet and Rivulet) would volunteer without a second thought. Khlainbor was quite sure of that. They were all sons of his father's ministers, the myntris, who had elected his father as the syiem, the chieftain of the hima. Later, they all campaigned successfully for him to become the MLA of the constituency and a minister. The golden period had lasted only three years. Before Badonbok Syiem could complete his full term he was killed in a road accident at the age of forty-three. Shocked and bewildered, his family and men retreated to the village, once again into a life of comparative anonymity and penury. Of that period of pain and anguish all that Khlain could clearly remember was the day his Meikha, his paternal grandmother, Aitimai Syiem, gathered the family around her and said, "Today is the third day after your father's funeral. The house has been aired and cleaned, the clothes washed and the prayers and rituals completed, thus mourning is over. We must now continue with life. I have lost a son and you, a father, what greater tragedy can there be? Still, let us take solace in the fact that the departed's life was an unblemished one. Let us be comforted by knowing that God took him away before greed and envy could claim him, before decadence and corruption could blacken his name, this son of mine who was brought up to always walk on the path of Truth, according to our religion and the rules laid down from time immemorial.

The myntris and the bakhraws, the nobles will now elect
a new syiem and we must all give them our full support
and loyalty."

Khlainbor went over the scene again and again. He
looked at the terraced slope showing signs of a promising
potato crop, the tiny flowers blooming white and the fields
of maize swaying in the breeze. In the distance he could
see the rolling hills covered with thick pine forests, young
trees and old trees rising gracefully from mother earth.
He suddenly felt faint and empty and took off his cap and
muffler and made a makeshift pillow and lay down on the
ground. From his back pocket he removed his pistol, the
only inheritance from his father, which he always carried
for safety, and placed it next to him. Then he kicked off
his keds and dipped his feet into the cool waters of the
little rivulet nearby and closed his eyes, deep in thought.
He thought for a long, long time.

How could he, Khlainbor Sing, actually call Aibor,
Madonlang, Duke and Earl and Pynsuk the sons of his
late father's Myntris and ask them to help smuggle red pine
from the reserved forests for the crass and greedy tycoon
from Shillong? Steal red pine by the truckload, so that the
man of new-found wealth can build his dream mansion to
match the homes of the affluent and aristocratic families
in town. Steal those precious trees. Steal and that too from
his father's hima. His grandmother's face, olive-toned and
calm, sailed over his thoughts like a little cloud as her
words reverberated through his soul. He thought of his
cousin, his father's sister's son, the present syiem, who
would wither away in shame at so terrible an act by a
family member. He could see each tree weeping and cursing
as it fell because of the enormity of the crime, the sadness

of the betrayal. "No," Khlainbor shouted. "No," to the sky
above and to the earth below. "I love you, Sinora. I really
do but ... we cannot lay the foundation of our home on
a mound of lies. I know you will understand.Of course
you will ... you will," he whispered, his pace quickening
towards home.

April sunsets were never spectacular like the monsoon
evening skies. That evening, however, the sky was an
unusual orange with grey-blue streaks and the hills
silhouetted against it like chunks of black onyx, glowed
with a strange luminescence. Khlainbor walked quickly
back to his village, light of heart and step, eager to share
his decision with his wife and sisters. He felt so elated. In
all his twenty-eight years he had not experienced such deep
nostalgia as he did that day.

His wife and sister were peeling potatoes and talking
animatedly when he arrived. He was surprised to see Joyla
there but when he saw the amount of pork sitting on the
table waiting to be cooked, he understood that Joyla and
her husband would also be dining with them that night.

Sinora saw him first and with absolute delight and
excitement in her voice said,

"You've come? Oh! I am so happy. Why don't you sit,
come."

"Bah! Why are you ... ? Is the work done? Si and I have
been waiting and waiting ... "

"Let's check his jacket. I am sure that's where the
treasure is, no Kong Joy?"

"The work is done isn't it Bah? Bah Heh ... "

Khlainbor controlled the confusion raging inside him
and with the greatest of effort focused on a tiny voice that
whispered again and again – on the path of truth, on the

path of truth. So before his sister could speak again and before he could waver, he looked straight ahead, beyond it all and replied, "No the work is not done and I have no treasure in my jacket."

Silence, dead silence crawled into the room and gripped it tight. The vegetable knives dropped from the women's hands and clattered on the floor. The kettle on the fire boiled and hissed, the water spilling onto the embers, silencing them forever. Khlainbor took one look at the bowed heads and headed for the door. He would go out, down to the pub. He would return only when he was totally drunk. His eyes smarted. He swallowed hard the despair and confusion that was beginning to overwhelm him one more time and kicked the door open.

Suddenly his sister screeched and so did his wife. Both of them – their voices criss-crossing and crackling like live wire, struck by lightning.

"This is expected of drunkards, nothing gets done, ever."

"If only you had got up early I am sure this wouldn't have happened."

"Drunkard, drunkard. Oh! Si I really pity you. Poor you. Poor you."

"I was so happy this morning Oh! Kong Joy what should we do, what should we do? All the people we have told ... "

"Bah how could you do this? Shame, shame, shame ... NO, NO, no more explanations. No more excuses ... "

Khlainbor blanked out.

Then it happened. It happened very quickly – just two shots, two straight shots. That was all and then ... and then the terrible howling of a man like an animal in great pain.

ASORPHI
SAN PHYLIS

There was only one relative whom Asorphi truly loved and respected and that was San Phylis, her mother's elder cousin. She lived in a large rambling house bought by her Anglo-Indian husband, an Air Force officer, when he retired and they moved to Upper Shillong. The house had an ample verandah with wooden railings painted white which encircled it like kindly arms. The house, although in obvious disrepair, had something welcoming and warm about it. To Asorphi it was her little oasis from all the storms and anxieties of her young life and also a place of fun and laughter.

After Richard Sanders succumbed to a long battle with cancer, San Phylis lived with her only child, her son, Jason. San Phylis taught English conversation, baking and flower arrangement. To whomever she thought was deserving enough she gave an extra half hour teaching the jive and fox-trot and ballroom dancing. People just loved those few hours with her; they had so much fun, like Asorphi.

Asorphi also loved the sights and sounds of this home full of books scattered on shelves, tables, chairs, all over the carpet – and the old radio that played music all day long – Khasi, Hindi, Western, and, of course, the hymns that are ever so soothing, so different. Asorphi thought San Phylis sang 'Ave Maria' like an angel.

Asorphi's home was quite different. Situated a few metres below on a tree-clad knoll it squatted resolutely, green-roofed, single-storied and very neat, very clean. It was her mother's house and since she was the only daughter, her husband moved in with her as was, and is, the custom in these hills. Every room in the house shone brass-bright like a new coin and every window had clean lace curtains that fluttered like moths, freshly winged. The little verandah in front had the usual pots of geraniums and roses on a wrought iron stand bought at an army fair. Two big pots of orchids took pride of place on either side of the main door. Flo, the daily help, removed dried leaves and wilted flowers every single day. Nothing was ever out of place; no one was ever out of sorts; a typical Khasi house. Her father saw to that.

Her father taught Khasi in a prominent college in town. He was always perfectly turned out in light suits all the year round with rich coloured pullovers worn discreetly inside, whenever the wind blew cold. He would step out at seven-thirty sharp every morning without any fuss. On the way to the bus stop he would nod pleasantly at all those he met, his short-cropped curly mop nicely oiled, his shoes polished and laced, his lessons for the day prepared and arranged methodically inside his head.

A few minutes later Asorphi's mother, fresh as a daisy, in a sober jainsem, the colour and print well suited for the Head Mistress of a recently opened and well-talked-about school in Rilbong, would board the waiting taxi. She and another teacher and three students of the same school had hired it over a year ago on a monthly basis. "We are so much more organized now" her mother had said, smiling quietly at her husband, knowing that he was mighty impressed. He did not approve of the fluster and rush each morning of those earlier days when she had to catch the school bus. It used to spoil his day and she knew it. In turn it spoilt her day as well.

Asorphi would hop in too, to be dropped off on the way at the Army School where she was finishing her twelfth. This routine went on uninterrupted day in and day out. Even the conversation inside the taxi between Kong Sil, her mother's friend, and her mother, never varied. "Well, well, do you think it is going to rain Ailin?"

"Kong Sil, I don't think so. Anyway, I have an umbrella, we can always share."

"No, no, it's all right. Did you watch Media Plus last night? Boring wasn't it?"

"Yes, and the screen, as usual shook so much. They should do something about it."

"Yes they should. I hope nothing crops up before Sunday. I really want to go for that church gathering in – ."

"Yes, I hope not. You really enjoy these outings don't you?" All that while, the three students kept a respectful silence, and Asorphi stared at the pine trees that lined the long and winding road that curved gently all the way down to the lower slopes of the town.

It was certainly no surprise that people in Shillong

were insecure about the weather and, therefore, obsessed by it. They would discuss it like anyone else would talk about important political developments and gruesome happenings. The weather in the eastern hill-station was exciting, moody, and unpredictable. In a day one could easily experience all four seasons. Still, Asorphi winced each time Kong Sil started on the topic.

So, one day, she decided to get it off her chest. After all, for how much longer could she divert her mind by counting the pine trees that lined the long and winding road, which had remained unchanged since she was a child? "Mei, why do you and Kong Sil discuss the weather every single day? I know she starts the topic but you can always put a stop to it ... after all you are the Head Mistress." Her mother looked up, her eyes widening, unable to answer as she had just bitten into a lettuce leaf, garden-fresh and crisp. Her father, as usual, came to his wife's rescue. "Asor, what else can two adults discuss in a car full of children? The weather is always the safest subject. Yes, your Mei is the Head Mistress but Kong Sil is senior in age and has to be given due respect. Mei knows what she is doing."

Of course she did. Asorphi watched her mother performing her duties meticulously – not only as a mother, wife and teacher but also as a sister, sister-in-law, aunt-in-law, daughter (when her mother was alive), daughter-in-law, cousin, friend, neighbour. She was so typical, like everybody else in that quiet, traditional locality. She had no single definite identity, there were so many selves merging into a fragmented whole, held loosely together like candy floss.

Asorphi shuddered at the thought with a certain amount of discomfort and disdain. She hoped her life would never

ever turn out like that. She would not get stuck to a man
like her father – dull, boring and grey like a winter's day.
As the words raced through her head and then slithered
down to her heart, she felt miserable and let down and
at the same time very guilty. From the corner of her eye
she looked at her father. He was chewing his food with
his mouth closed, as one should, totally oblivious of her
thoughts. Asorphi quietly sighed with relief and stretched
out for some more slices of roast pork when he interrupted
her, "Take the fish curry khun, take the full head and suck
out the brain, it's very good for you. See Bengalis are so
intelligent because they love their morighonto! Have it,
have it, you will like the taste, you always did. It's very
good for the brain."

Asorphi served herself some fish head curry as
recommended as she glared at the glass bowl full of salad
wishing that it would suddenly fall. How she wished it
would, so that the table would be strewed with tomatoes,
fresh green chilies and pearly white onions. Then she could
playfully tug at her father's arm and have a great big laugh,
just the way San Phylis did when Rudolph bit into a juicy
Delhi Mistan Bhandar 'jalebi' and dropped syrup all over
his tie and shirt. She longed to escape into such delightful,
refreshing chaos.

San Phylis was so different, so definite. She was simply
Phylisdora Kharkongor. Full stop. While her husband was
alive the letters and cards were, of course, addressed to
Mrs & Squadron Leader Richard Sanders. "Even during
those years I was Mrs Sanders only on paper and would
always introduce myself as Phylis Kharkongor. Your uncle,
Richard loved it especially when the people around would
gasp and gape and ask 'Why not Phylis Sanders?' I wouldn't

give a straight answer about our matrilineal system etc. – the usual stuff you know. I would teasingly say, 'Why not Richard Kharkongor?' It was great fun, Asor. There was another instance when a certain Mrs Bhatnagar said to me at a party in Agra, in the middle of a discussion about where everyone came from and the usual topics in such gatherings, 'So it means you have no caste.' And I replied, 'Yes, the way you have no class.' There was pin-drop silence in the room as I continued to sip my juice very calmly and casually as if nothing had transpired. Very soon the conversation picked up again as if really and truly nothing had happened. Remember, there is no one and nothing which is too big or too small; nothing is that important or unimportant in life. Everyone and everything has its own place and relevance, remember and respect that fact – always. Come let's have some tea and carrot cake and watch the sunset from the verandah. You are looking a little washed out today. What's the matter, Asor baieit? Would you like to tell me?"

A day with San Phylis would progress like that. Hand in hand she would walk out with her aunt and inhale the fragrance of wet grass and quiet thoughts. Jason would be playing the piano. His version of 'Sohlyngngem', a Khasi folk song, would float out of the house into the fading light. Asorphi would sip her tea looking at her aunt watching the sky, relishing each moment of this special time with Aunt Phylis: her refuge from the prosaic and claustrophobic atmosphere at home. Strange, how her aunt always seemed to know when there was something wrong. Even when just one little note was out of tune in anyone's inner music, she would guess and try to put it right.

It was Sunday and Asorphi's parents, who were not

converts but still believed in the indigenous faith, Niam Khasi, had gone down to town to attend the annual general meeting of the Seng Khasi. It was almost the end of the year and the Seng Kut Snem celebrations were nearing and the programme had to be chalked out. As they drove off in their perfectly maintained Maruti Zen, Asorphi wished with all her heart that she was in the car too and that they were all going for a picnic to Barapani to enjoy the sun and the songs and laughter of other picnickers beside the lake. There was only one alternative – spend the day with San Phylis and confide her disappointment.

She had a quick bath, slipped into a skirt and blouse and headed for her aunt's house. She found her amidst her salvias with the wizened gardener, smiling in the late morning sun. Of course, as usual she knew. Asorphi poured her heart out, squirming with embarassment at the thought of her having to confide her opinion about her father.

"It's nothing serious, San Phylis, it's just my parents ..."

"Your parents?"

"Yes, I love them and all that sort of thing ... but they are so, I don't know what to say, I just find them so dull ..."

"Dull and sober are too different things, Asor sweetheart."

"The house is like a tomb, San."

"Don't you have fun here?"

"Of course, of course I do."

"So that's your share of fun in life. Everyone is given a share of everything, in its own place, in its own time. You don't have to get everything from one person and one place. Your mother's branch of the family was and is always very correct and sober and I think your father and mother are so well suited. No one's the same, darling. You don't see the same birds in the trees, the same flowers and trees in the garden ... look around, see. Don't just look – see, don't just hear – listen. Whatever exists in nature is replicated in our lives, that is why we say what is natural is the best. Anyway, tell me ... "

"My mother, well, she is, I suppose, quite normal. she has some good times with her friends in school, in her social work, even in the locality activities, but Pa, he's so ... I don't know... I just want to shake him ... he is not natural," Asorphi cried out feeling so guilty, so disloyal but distraught and at the same time very curious. "San, what was Pasan like? Uncle Richard? What was he like? I wish he was here he would have taught my father a thing or two! San Phylis? San Phylis? Oh! I am so sorry to have upset you. Did I say something wrong? Well, frankly I don't care anymore. I am so tired. Pa is a dull, exasperating man and I know you think so too. Why don't you say it?"

Phylis Kharkongor stared at her niece in a way which Asorphi found strange, uncharacteristic and, therefore, disconcerting. As she stretched out to touch her aunt's caftan, Phylis suddenly walked away so quickly that it left Asorphi stranded in a pool of complete bewilderment. She stood rooted to the ground very still, completely stunned. Then she ran after her aunt across the lawn, into the verandah and then into the house.

The house was quiet except for the sound of the shower in San Phylis' bathroom. The sound of water seemed to go on and on, just the sound of water and nothing else. She curled up on the sofa and waited. Deep inside she knew that it was a special day, different. All will be well. She was in San Phylis' house.

It took a while before San Phylis emerged. Just a quiet smile and then she sat next to her niece. She seemed a little different, like someone who needed to visit a beauty salon. She looked wan, dishevelled as she began to brush her hair absent-mindedly, on and on. Asorphi looked down at her toes and not knowing what to do next, she started to cry.

Phylis Kharkongor turned and gathered her niece in her arms and held her close to her heart, stroking her hair till the tears subsided. Finally, after a long time she spoke; her words flowing out quietly, haltingly like a river that had lost its way.

"Sweetheart, this is not an easy story … you see, your father is a childhood friend of the entire family. He is an absolutely wonderful man. Sure he is not fun but …he is solid, you know. It was because of the stability he provided that your mother, my gentle cousin, was able to blossom and I … I was able to fly. I, too, was in love with him, Asorphi. We were close. Then I went away to Calcutta for an advance training course in Nursing. I was twenty-four. One day your father … he proposed to your mom … and she accepted. I got the news and I wept. I … I was already carrying his child and didn't know what to do but I was sure I wanted to carry the baby, to give birth to the baby. I simply did not think twice about that although it was a mistake. After all, deep inside I knew he was in love with your mother and yet I … well what had to happen happened. No one can change that Asor. What happened was an accident and a lucky one isn't it? Now where was I? Oh yes! I managed to get my first posting far away in the South. You ... were born there. You were the sweetest child in the world. When you were two months old your parents came and your mother asked me if she could adopt you as she had been told that she couldn't have a child. I agreed. Asor, you are my child. That is why we connect the way we do that is why we find so much joy in each other. You are brought up by ... by ... your mother but you are my child. I am your Meisan, your elder mother. How lucky you are, you have two moms! Soon after I accepted my most ardent admirer's proposal, your Uncle Richard! Jason was born a year later."

Time stood still for Asorphi. Nothing moved as her aunt's words spread all over her like healing balm. An enormous cloud lifted from her head; she could almost see it bobbing away like a little balloon. She felt light and free. She did not either shout and scream or faint with the surprise and joy of the revelation.

Perhaps it was because she always knew.

BETIMAI
THE PASSING

His going had to be different. I woke up some time in the middle of the night to the onslaught of a cold wind that had pushed the window open. As I struggled to shut it the fragrance of sweet peas assailed my senses and mingled with the smell of death.

It didn't take me long to decide that I should wait till the morning. He would prefer it that way. He disliked scenes as much as he disliked causing any kind of inconvenience to anyone. He was kind and cultured. He belonged to the town's best family, although a black sheep to some because he became an alcoholic and did not 'make it' in life – which to most meant that he neither made money nor a great career. To me he was the most successful man in town because he was good and kind to me.

I was his fourth wife and I loved him dearly. We had no children and my mother mourned the misfortune of her youngest daughter for over a year until he charmed her beyond reprieve. Besides, by then my middle sister had produced a third daughter, the loveliest of them all. Mei was more than reassured that the family lineage was secure. Still, as you know, aging people keep repeating themselves. So she would, off and on, sing her refrain, "Bettimai, people who drink cannot father children. How unfortunate! Shish, Shish, how unfortunate!" This would, inevitably, be followed by a smile in her eyes as she would recall that her youngest son-in-law was an aristocrat. I knew what was in her mind because she would glance at me lovingly and with approval. I would then quickly add, "You have four grandchildren from your daughters. Your sons-in-law are also special. The elder one is an engineer, the second one is a charismatic MLA and the third is such a good man." Mei's smile would spread to the rest of her face for she always liked to see the brighter side of things. She would nod and end with, "And *My* son is an IAS officer. One day he will become a DC!" We would both smile at each other, content: Mei, the youngest daughter of her generation and me, the khadduh of the present.

When I met my husband he had taken premature retirement from his government job and was working for a local newspaper as special assistant editor. He would contribute occasional articles on health, culture, travel and other topics, staying studiously away from politics. The proprietor of the newspaper never pressured him about anything. He, too, liked and respected him. Of course he didn't earn much. I loved him all the same. I loved the way he would quietly sip his tea in the morning, read the newspapers, his old and frayed dressing gown, elegantly sheathing his slim body. Not everyone had such expensive pyjama suits and dressing gowns. Some had none at all.

It was not traditional wear and just as foreign as the breakfast he relished: porridge or cornflakes with milk, toast and eggs and fruit, while the rest of us ate boiled rice, meat stew, fried fish and salad. Those who worked packed whatever they wanted in their lunch boxes. When we had relatives from afar staying over or morning guests he would say, "Please don't make a fuss about food. We'll all eat together. I would like to have some rice and meat stew for a change. I even saw dal being cooked. Don't fuss about my breakfast all right?" But Mei would do just that. She liked it because he was different and she knew everyone else did too. So he would be served his usual fare with a cup of red tea and a slice of lemon. He would be served in a different room like a prince.

He was special. The way he treated me and my family and friends, the neighbourhood, my belongings, his belongings, the way he conducted himself even when he was drunk was so different. There was a distinct refinement in the way he talked, walked, ate and dressed. Sometimes I would wonder how he would make love and I would blush at the thought. I would feel so disloyal and selfish because he had, after all, confessed to me and confirmed my mother's fears that he was impotent because of excessive drinking. I had told him that it did not matter. I was nearing forty and didn't know what it was like to be touched in such a way by a man and I had accepted it as part of my destiny. Each day I counted my other blessings, each year, eight in all.

His cirrhotic liver, however could not hold on and had turned cancerous. When the doctors informed him of the prognosis, he accepted it with no remorse. "Let it be as God wills it" he said. He fought bravely for many months and now he was finally gone. I dragged my quilt to the divan, settled the cushions and tried to sleep. I knew what I had to do when I got up. I had already thought about it. In the eight years as his wife I had learnt to live like him and not panic because everything had to happen the way it was meant to and we had to cope with faith and dignity. So I tried to sleep, settling my thoughts into some kind of order. I didn't want to bungle things and falter during the next few days. I wanted everything to go off smoothly the way he would have liked.

I couldn't sleep, waiting for dawn with a corpse in my room, although I was quite sure that he was waiting along with me, in spirit. He must have known that I was doing what I was only for his sake, for his comfort and peace. It wasn't time, after all, for the world to be astir and the thought of crowds of mourners disturbing the stillness seemed abhorrent to me.

When the first streaks of dawn lit the sky I tiptoed to his side. Strangely enough his eyes were closed. I touched his forehead gently again and again as tears sprang up from the depths of my being and slid down my face, my neck, soaking into my jainkyrshah with a few drops falling on my feet. I stood there for quite a while till all the sorrow had drained and I had nothing left to tell him. "Go in peace, leit suk, and thank you for the eight wonderful years." I whispered, looking around the room, wondering where his soul was lodged. I tidied the room meticulously before I opened the window to let the fresh air in. It came sweeping in bringing in the confetti of peach blossoms as if nature was determined to be the first to pay her respects to him along with me. When the room was filled with freshness I closed the window and stepped out into the world of the living.

I went to the kitchen and made three cups of tea for the three of us, Mei, the daily help and myself. The tray with a tea set of white china with a blue-band design and a matching tea cozy lay on the kitchen counter. I opened the back door for the maid to enter and putting two cups of steaming hot tea on a tray, I walked down the corridor to Mei's room. I knocked and waited a second before I opened the door. She was combing her hair and I let her finish before I put the cups down on her table. Her heater was on. Once March was over, however, she would not dream of drinking tea in her room. Eating and drinking in the bedroom was not done unless one was ill.

I let her finish her tea and then I broke down and told her. She wept softly, filling the room with sadness. "Khun, we should have taken some photographs last night. There were some shots left in the camera. Everyone was here for dinner and he looked so relaxed and handsome... and now he is gone. Ring up your sisters and brother and..."

"Yes, Mei, I know" and I rushed out of the room to do just that: to inform my closest ones to spread the sad news that my husband was dead. The maid heard my conversation over the phone and, sobbing, went out to inform the neighbours.

When I re-entered Mei's room she had opened the tall almirah and was studying each dhara thoughtfully. We took out his favourite colours, two mukas, the soft beige glow bordered with white, and a navy blue, a grey and a deep maroon as well. On the mosquito net stand of my bed we hung them up to screen the body before the mourners arrived. I hung the mukas at the foot of the bed, the blue and grey on either side. The wall behind the bed had two framed pictures on it. We kept the maroon one to cover the coffin. I didn't turn the pictures on their backs. Mei didn't allow me to turn any photograph around as was normally done. All the photographs with smiling faces and the pictures with happy scenes remained untouched, staring from the walls like an audience.

The neighbours arrived in droves along with my mother's cousin who lived next door. Some of the children had decided to miss school to come and mourn with me and help with the tea and kwai and small errands. Then my brother arrived with his family and my mother's only surviving cousin brother, my mama. Then came the group from the Seng Khasi that was in charge of making the krong and all the other necessary arrangements for the funeral. My sisters took over the rest of the tasks. The velvet had to be bought for the cover to screen the pyre during the cremation. The shanduwa with tassels made of wool, some beaten silver set into the tips would be prepared for the siar kait. Gold too had to be procured for a ring and a chain that he would wear to be burnt along with his body and left with the ashes to be collected by the nongkylla thang, the people who see that the mortal remains were properly and completely incinerated. I saw my mother handing money to my elder sister which was, I presume, for the tea and kwai and the meals that would have to be served to relatives and friends who came from afar and the many who came to help and sleep over at our house. Of course many had brought their contribution, rice, sugar, tea, biscuits, fruit, words of comfort and support.

It was decided that his body would be kept for one night and the funeral would be at 2 p.m. the following day: at this time the funeral procession would proceed from the house to the cremation ground. Before that each person would come up to pay his or her last respects. First the khas, his family members from the father's side, always highly respected because the father is responsible for one's birth after all. Kha means to give birth. Then the spouse and children would come next followed by the kur (the clan), those he belonged to, according to tradition, from the time of his birth to the last moments of his life on earth.

All day people came and went. Inside, wherever there was space mulas and benches were placed for people to sit. Outside chairs and more benches dotted the garden where men had gathered, making small talk and holding serious discussions on whatever suited their interests. It is understood that once the formal condolences are over usually no one speaks of the dead. He had, after all, returned to the house of God, 'iing U Blei, according to His will. In the garden shed a makeshift kitchen had been set up for making cups of tea and preparing food. People's voices, muffled and quiet, hummed along with the breeze in the trees and the chirping of birds. I sat in the room where his body lay, on a mattress on the ground, while he lay in our bed curtained by the carefully chosen mukas and dharas. Thus the day slipped by into a night of waiting.

Inside my room, ladies took turns to stay up with me. Outside, around a bonfire the menfolk sat up, sipping their tea and drinks, telling stories to pass their time. I drifted in and out of sleep remembering. I remembered the last movie we watched, the enchanting trip to the Jaintia Hills to the monolith park and to the Kali Puja thereafter. The photographs had come out so well. In front of the tallest monolith, over 70 metres high, we laughed as we commented how we looked like dwarves and beside the ancient idols of Kali we resembled displaced giants. I remembered the laughter that the photographs evoked. I thought of the little tremors inside me during that drive –strangely, the first and last we did—without family and friends. It was enchanting. A few days later his cancer was detected. I was trying to eat my dinner. He noticed my trembling hands and said from across the table, "Enjoy your meal. It is very important to enjoy one's food… and listen … never fear because there is nothing that one can fear that has not already happened, no feeling that one can feel that one has not already experienced. It is just a question of remembering. That is what they mean when they say 'be prepared'." Thus with the memories of such rich and happy days the night glided into yet another day. Yet it wasn't any other day.

My mother took out more muka jainsems for me and my sisters, old ones, slightly frayed to suit the occasion. My middle sister insisted that she wouldn't change but would stick to her grey silk jainsem. My elder sister decided she would wear the oldest and most sober muka from Mei's collection. I don't remember what Mei wore but I chose to wear my favourite one, my great- grandmother's muka which was a hundred years old and had long, very long tassels. I wanted to look good and exceptional when I accompanied him on his last journey.

By one o'clock, the priest had arrived wearing an off-white turban with his brown shiny suit and pointed shoes. Gone were the days of dhotis and collared jackets that went so well with the elegant turban. He sat near the bed on a mula and looked around the room and asked no one in particular, loudly and clearly, "Should we start?" Everyone looked at my mother and she, in turn, glanced at her closest clansman, my mama, who replied, "All right, do let us begin." The decision was forwarded all over, to the people in the various rooms, outside in the garden and some who were having a break in the neighbour's houses.

On my insistence, as the fourth wife, I asked that his clan come first. First his mother came with her clan, his clan, his kur. Then the khas, the paternal side, came next. They lined up and one by one walked up to the priest who announced his or her name and relationship with the dead after which the relatives muttered words of farewell, of affection, or whatever they wished. Before walking away some contribution in cash was given to the priest. He in turn put the money which would eventually go to the nongkyllathang, on a piece of white cloth placed next to the body. The money from the clan was placed on the right and the amount from the khas and all gathered there on the left. His khas were a sombre lot with long, dark faces and big hands and feet typical of the elaka they came from. My turn came next along with the rest of my family and clan. I touched his head and re-arranged his hair. I had nothing more to say but I could feel him looking at me from somewhere in the room filled with admiration and love, the best combination of feelings a woman could ever hope for from the man she loved. I returned to me place on the ground.

Soon after I heard the priest saying, "This is your first wife from the Myrthong clan and your two children." She must have been a truly beautiful woman once. She reminded me of Wallis Simpson, the famous Duchess of Windsor. Her two sons looked a lot like her. There was no significant trace of him except in their slightly bushy eyebrows and the younger one's hair, stubborn curls that refused any tempering. All three paid their respects and moved on. They were followed by his second family, the Marbaniangs from West Khasi Hills. The wife had passed away so his daughter came with her aunt, her mother's sister. She was a pretty child and would have had a perfect face if only her nose was not so much like his, far too prominent for a girl. His third family seemed a trifle too loud in their dressing and demeanor. I couldn't look at them because firstly, they were reeking of a strong smelling hair oil and I felt they nursed a grudge against me as he had left their mother to marry me. Besides, their clan was known to be the worshippers of U Thlen who also dabbled in black magic. The younger child's shoes squeaked as he walked past. I winced and put my head on my knees hiding my feelings and my face. I braced myself for the next lot, his clan. I was looking forward to seeing his tall and elegant mother, always perfectly turned out, and his sisters who were very dignified and well groomed yet affable and gracious to everyone. His younger brother was my favourite, full of life, intelligent and at that time engaged to his future wife. She was a singer of considerable repute, part Naga and part Mizo who sang 'Forever Young' on my husband's last birthday. I was waiting for them when there was buzz in the room, which snapped me out of my reverie.

A woman had entered the room with an elderly man and a young boy, who was barely four years old. She must have been a little over twenty, petite with a pert, pleasant face streaked with tears. The priest muttered the formalities while they paid their last respects and handed over their contribution. I was wondering who they were when my best friend; a younger cousin sidled up to me and held me by the shoulder. They turned to leave and the lady and her chaperone stopped for a second in front of Mei and me and my sisters condoling wordlessly, heads bowed. The boy followed and as he passed me his little face was the same height as mine and our eyes met. In that one instant I knew whose son he was and why he had come. I knew who the lady was and why she had come. I was also quite sure by then that the little boy was not more than four or five years old. I had been married for eight years, eight without any physical intimacy because by his own admission he had "a problem".

My heart tried to sink but I wouldn't let it. I took a deep breath and said to the little one clearly and loudly so that all those present would hear and be at peace, "You look so much like your father, little one. God bless you."

DONDORLIN
ROSALYNN

We stumbled upon the grave by accident that afternoon. Shalini and I were looking for a place to rest awhile and catch our breath when we saw a bit of it, a bit of white that gleamed through the almost impenetrable growth around it like a hidden eye. I picked up a thick twig and tried to remove the pine cones and fallen leaves and the anonymous remnants of dead vegetation that had accumulated for years and years, perhaps even for centuries.

"Good heavens, Dondor, it is a grave," Shalini exclaimed, staring wide-eyed at the flat piece of marble at our feet. It was obviously an old forgotten grave: the arch that must have once stood guard at its head had succumbed to the onslaught of mountain winds and rain. The words on the slab were still somewhat visible though, gazing at us in black and white.

"Rosalynn Anne … " the words tumbled out of me effortlessly. "A beautiful name for a beautiful woman, she really was beautiful."

Shalini gasped. I turned to look at her. Her face was completely drained of colour, her eyes liquid with fear. It was only then that the full impact of what I had just said hit me. Horror clung to me in a cold sweat and my legs felt as weak as straw.

"Let's get out of here," Shalini whispered. "Come, on fast!" I could feel her pull my hand.

We ran for the second time that day. We ran as fast as our legs could carry us, crunching the autumn leaves beneath our feet into tiny pieces.

* * *

We had arrived in K two days before that, just as the sun was setting. The hills, the valleys, the whole earth and the sky were steeped in pink. The scene was so much like a late. August Shillong evening after a heavy afternoon shower. I felt a certain ache in my heart and wished the bus was lumbering up the road just after Sumer and soon we would reach the Barapani Lake and then home.

"Here we are!" Shalini's cheery voice broke my reverie. The bus had halted near the little marketplace as the sun began to disappear and the sky turned into a deep orange. Slowly dusk came filtering in, its uncertain light blurring the entire landscape. The lights come on in the shops, highlighting a charming cobbled road that traversed the bazaar. Himachali scarves and jackets, so typical of the place, hung cheerfully, vying for pride of place with the billowing chunnis. I knew I wasn't home.

"We should have taken the night train. We would have been here early morning," Shalini said, apprehensive as she watched the darkness hastening in.

Not that I blamed her for worrying, for she had been the master-mind behind our little trip up to K. when Delhi University had closed down for three days because of a student union strike. The heat, which had just about dissipated, had left us sapped of all our energy. I was missing Shillong terribly, aching for the cold, invigorating air and the sound of the crickets in the hedges, the lowing of the cows on a distant hill.

Shalini had never been to K. before but she knew that her maternal grandfather had a house called 'Skye End' at the end of Wavell Road. Sitting in our hostel room smoking cheap cigarettes, we became completely intoxicated by the name of the house and the thought of the distant hills. Only then we thought it was 'sky' not skye. Ruby and Neera backed out at the last minute because their boyfriends had other plans. So Shalini and I packed a small rucksack each of clothes and toiletries and left by the morning bus.

The bus rolled into the bus stop which had little tea stalls and magazine stands, throbbing with life. The sight lifted our spirits a little. We jumped off the bus and stretched our limbs, jogging energetically much to the amusement of our co-passengers.

"From which country?" one of them asked.

"From faraway," I replied wearily.

"Accha," he said, nodding and took great pride in informing everyone.

They all smiled and walked away. Foreigners were always forgiven their eccentricities. We really did not care at that point in time. We, from faraway, were desperately looking for some kind of transport to get to our destination. In front of a fabric shop, where the most colourful village prints were proudly displayed, stood a solitary rickshaw.

"Shalini, quick, there's a rickshaw there," I said, and quickened my pace towards it. "Wavell Road, how far?" I asked the rickshawallah.

"Almost a kilometre," he responded, eyeing us with the typical curiosity of a small towner. "You from Bangkok?"

"No," thundered Shalini. "We are Indians, we've come from Delhi. We won't give you a single extra penny. Let's go bhaiya, let us go."

"After dark I charge extra," was the calm reply of the hillman, as he lit a 'bidi' leisurely.

"All right, we understand that," I intervened calmly, glaring at Shalini to check her from bursting into typical North Indian aggressiveness. This time, I knew, it wasn't going work. She realized it too.

We climbed on before he could change his mind. I was so relieved that we had found some conveyance, I would have paid double and cut on some other expense. After two years in Delhi I had learnt to be very careful about not roaming around unescorted after dark. Even during the day the men were blatant: trying to rub against our bodies in marketplaces and busy roads, propositioning and exhibiting themselves in lonely spots. The rickshaw bounced along on the cobbled road and then turned into a narrow path lined on either side with silver oaks.

A couple of old street lamps winked wearily before we found ourselves suddenly on a moonlit road that dissected a pine scented forest into two.

"Thank God! There's a moon tonight," I exclaimed.

"Wavell Road," the old man hollered.

"Carry on, the house is at the end of the road," Shalini shouted back as the night breeze ruffled her hair in all directions. She had never seen the house before. She knew, however, that it was built on a sort of promontory at the end of Wavell Road, where the sky dipped into the valley below.

"Where?" the rickshawallah asked. He stopped, suddenly still as a tomb.

"Skye End that's the name of the house," Shalini answered, her voice rising above the mounting night wind.

"Skye End ... " the rickshawallah whispered and in spite of the darkness the fear and shock in his voice was almost tangible.

"Yes, it's my grandfather's house and we are going to stay there," Shalini replied, too excited to notice what I had.

"I can't go there" the old man retorted in a tone of unwavering finality as he turned his rickshaw around.

"Why? What do you mean?" Shalini jumped off the rickshaw and stormed towards him.

"I can't. There's no proper road leading to the house. It's not far now. You can easily walk it ... if you wish to go there," he said.

"We won't pay you. After all ... " I intervened hoping to change his mind before Shalini burst into one of her famous tirades.

"Don't. I am going," he countered and before we could say another word he had disappeared into the night.

I looked at Shalini. There was a hint of fear and bewilderment on her face which she quickly dismissed.

"Come along, Dondor, he said it isn't far," she stated bravely and I followed her like a loyal soldier. There really was no other alternative.

The forest of pine reminded me of the upper reaches of Shillong, its aroma assailed my senses. I quickly swallowed all the emotions that were threatening to engulf me. The moment was important, there was no time for nostalgia. I knew that the more positive Shalini and I were, the better the outcome. The past should never intrude into the present or the present into the future.

There must have been a road there once that stretched like a white ribbon right up to the house. Nature, however, had obviously triumphed in her "quiet, perfidious way" and the path gradually gave way to an undefined mess choked with pariah shrubs and plants. The sickly sweet smell of lantana crept to our noses, intensifying the atmosphere of gross neglect, death and decay. I remember the trees above our heads, their long branches like the gnarled fingers of an aged witch, which entwined to form a vault. The wind, now soft and stealthy, coursed through these branches like whispers in secret corridors.

My mind travelled back to one moonlit November night in school. Since we were in our last year the nuns permitted us to study for as long as we wished in the library. At 10 pm the bearers would serve us hot chocolate and cookies as we pored over our books in a last ditch effort to produce desired results. I had stayed back all by myself that one night struggling with my History course. It was well after midnight and past lights-out time so I crouched on the one single sofa which was near a window and raced through the pages with the moonlight streaming in through the window panes. Suddenly the wind started its journey through the trees and brought the sound of footsteps so similar to the ones I was hearing now in the dark forest thousands of miles away in time and place. I pursed my lips and looked heavenwards and prayed that the similarity should end there. I would not be able to go through what occurred soon after in that moon-washed library two days before my History exam.

"Dondor, are you all right?"

"Huh? What happened?" her question dragged me back is the present.

"Your hands have suddenly become clammy and cold. Don't be scared ya ... "

"No, no I'm not," I lied. "I was just remembering something ... " I realized that Shalini was holding my hand.

"What? Come on, let's hear your little story. It'll divert us ... "

"No, no Shal – another day. I promise."

It was soon after this interlude that we reached 'Skye End.' The house suddenly presented itself to us, framed against the sky like a many-headed monster. It was huge, built like a chateau, its many windows, unlit, unused, glowered down at us like sightless eyes.

"Well, here we are," Shalini sighed with relief. "Come, let's go to the back. I believe the staff lives there."

We tramped across the dew-drenched grass, which touched our knees and tickled. Long, long ago it must have been a well-tended lawn, smooth and manicured, cornered with beds of the choicest flowers.

"It's a massive place Shalini," I remarked, looking up at the house, I was fatigued and groggy yet I was sure I saw a figure leaning from one of the balconies and then withdrawing hastily into the dark. Shalini, however, was saying, "I don't know why that rickshawallah was so scared to come here. We have, after all, reached safe and sound," so I kept quiet and refrained from telling her what I had just seen.

At the back of the house a small tin-roofed cottage squatted under an old walnut tree. It was lamplit, its gentle light escaping into the dark through a tiny window. Shalini walked quickly ahead. I held back with bated breath. I saw her knock.

"Who's there?" a voice hoarse with age, responded in Hindi.

Shalini moved to the window and said something I couldn't hear. She must have told the voice who she was because presently the door creaked open and a short, bent man emerged. I hurried forward and joined them. He was Nepali and introduced himself as Dhan Bahadur.

"Yes, yes," he commented, "I have heard of your mother, our saheb's only daughter, but ... I've never seen her ... She ... "

"Yes, she never came here because this is where my Nana's special friend lived. I know all that." Shalini quickly swept away the old man's embarrassment.

"You are most welcome, come, come," he muttered happily, relieved.

"We'd like a room upstairs with a good view," Shalini told him, as if she was booking into a hotel. Well 'Skye End' was far bigger than most small-town hotels.

"Yes, yes" he nodded, smiling. "I will give you quilts too. I just sunned them today, the pillows too ... and the sheets and towels are washed. My wife ... " he stopped thoughtfully for a moment, then continued, "My wife said to me 'the fire is crackling so much there will be visitors. For over thirty years ever since ...' "

"I know," Shalini held him by his shoulder, comforting him. "Dhan Bahadur we have not come here to be sad and to judge anyone. Let's go upstairs. We will talk about it tomorrow. We will share stories tomorrow."

Shalini's grandfather deserted the house and moved back to Delhi when his young Scottish mistress died suddenly. Years after the tragedy his brothers persuaded him to put the house up for sale. After much coaxing Siddharth Rai agreed and left the entire operation in Shalini's mother's hands. Aunty Priya told me that her decision was swift for there were no emotions involved, she did not know either the Scottish lady or her mother, Indira Rai, who died when she was two years old. So she decided that from the substantial amount expected from the sale of the house she'd give half to her widowed mami who had two daughters and a spastic son, who had been the kindest and closest relative she knew. It all sounded very fair and wise and her father readily agreed, understanding very well his daughter's inborn desire to always do some good and appease the demons she had had to face. Instead of the quick and profitable sale that was expected however, strange happenings occurred. The two serious buyers who had started negotiations with the Rais suffered massive heart attacks and had to back out. A third one, a hotelier, who had come all the way from Bangalore met with an accident on his way back from Shimla. Aunty Priya shelved the idea and had never revived it. She was far from keen about our trip up to K but who could ever stop Shalini from doing what she wanted?

We were given a room on the first floor, which faced
north towards Shimla, the capital town. It looked beautiful
with the star-spangled sky illuminating the distant hill-
tops. While Dhan Bahadur made the beds and settled the
room, we went to the verandah and stretched ourselves on
the long-armed easy chairs. I unpacked our meagre dinner
of buns, boiled eggs and cheese cubes with end of-the-
season mangoes for dessert. We ate in silence and gratitude,
enveloped in our own thoughts. The entire day, for me, had
been fraught with strange sights and sounds and I went to
bed early, my head filled with receding stars.

I woke up next morning to the songs of the birds in the
trees. I imagined that it was very early but when I opened
my eyes, the autumn sun was strong and warm and poured
in through the curtains of fraying silk.

"Lazybones," Shalini called out "I was up ages back,
so I sat and scribbled a few postcards to my cousins from
Skye End! They will be so excited to get one from here.
Let's have some tea or do you want to gargle?"

"Tea please," I replied yawning. It was only when I tried
to get up that I realized that my legs were wobbly and my
head was reeling.

"Hey! I think I've got mild fever. See, just check," I
told Shalini.

"Yes, you have … just when I'd got the whole day
planned out. Never mind let's have tea and I'll go off for
a walk to town while you rest. Isn't it absolutely beautiful
here?" Shalini's eyes grew misty. I looked at her but couldn't
read her thoughts.

After I had washed we sipped our tea which was a little
too strong and far too sweet, but welcome all the same.
Actually nothing could have ruined the exquisite aura of

peace and beauty around us. Shalini left, promising to bring back some crocins and magazines and pick up something interesting for dinner. An unopened carton of orange juice and the cheese sandwiches we had packed from the bus stop would make a great brunch for me, I told her, as she breezed off in her inimitable, buoyant style.

"Don't worry ya, just go and have a great day," I said.

I sat with my feet in the sun, observing the garden below and journeyed back into time. I saw the lawn smooth and green like a billiard table and the flower beds bursting with colour, just like the gardens of Shillong in late spring. I imagined a scene in the old days, in the early evenings when the host and hostess of Skye End and their guests would all sit under the shade of the spreading oak tree and wait for tea. A liveried bearer would arrive with a tray of fine white china cups patterned with pink blossoms, another with a tray with a silver tea set and yet another carrying cucumber sandwiches, hot chicken patties and a walnut cake. After tea they would walk across the lawn into the forest of pine, casting long shadows in the lambent light. I wondered what Siddharth Rai looked like when he was young and I tried to picture his foreign mistress who nobody in Shalini's family had ever seen.

I was twiddling my sun-warmed toes, still daydreaming when I spotted someone walking in the lawn. She was a small woman, fortyish maybe, and from her blouse of crimson velvet and the bright coloured beads around her neck, I guessed she was Nepali. The chowkidar's wife, I decided, the one who Dhan Bahadur said had heard the 'fire crackling'. She was engaged in some kind of activity and I struggled to my feet and peered down with more concentration. She walked to one corner of the overgrown lawn and her hands began to move as if she was picking flowers. Then clutching the imaginary bunch in her hands she walked back towards the main house wading through the tall grass. By then I realized my fever had gone up. I munched two Marie biscuits and washed down a crocin with a glass of orange juice before getting back into bed and drifting off to sleep.

I do not know how long I had slept before I woke up to the sound of movement in the next room. I could hear the rustling of silk and someone humming a song, with an unfamiliar lilt, which trickled into my room like a little stream.

I was very weak but my fever was gone. I tiptoed out of the room into the back verandah that semi-circled the entire first floor with stairs leading down from both ends. I followed the sound, which led me to a door two rooms away from mine. The door was ajar, the pleasing fragrance of lavender wafted out with the breeze. The curtain had disintegrated with age and hung on bravely from the thick brass rings of ornate design. Not being able to contain my curiosity I found myself looking into the room.

A woman stood framed against the window that looked out into the distant range of clouds and snow. Her hair, the colour of ripened corn, fell gently down to her waist. She was still singing softly – the song I had heard like the passing of water over little pebbles, a song of her home far, far away.

This continued for a few minutes. I don't quite recollect how long actually and then, to my rising excitement, she moved. She edged towards the gilded mirror and her face, small and exquisite, fell into it like a lost star into a startled pond. I moved towards the door. How happy she would be to see me, I thought, for she looked very lonely and sad. I was about to knock when my head suddenly reeled as I swayed and plunged into total darkness.

When I regained consciousness and opened my eyes, Shalini's face hung over me like an ailing moon.

"Dondor, how are you? Why were you wandering in the corridor? You gave me the fright of my life. Dhan Bahadur had to come and do his bit, jhaarphook or whatever he called it for you to stop raving and ranting. You crazy goof ... you sure gave me a scare ya ... Hey! Why are you staring like that? Dondor?"

"Shalini, I saw a woman two rooms away she was ... "

"WHAT? Stop it Don. It's the fever ... "

"No, it wasn't."

"Dondorlin Tham, you are always imagining things. What were you saying about the time when you were in your School Library? Tell me ... "

"You are trying to divert me. Okay, I'll tell you both the stories ... about then and now. It was past bedtime and I was studying all by myself in the library by moonlight when the wind began to blow and then I heard someone moaning outside. At first I thought it was the wind ..."

"It must have been the wind passing through the trees ... "

"I thought so too till the next afternoon when we heard that Farah, the girl from the family across the road had died the previous night at her husband's home in Kuwait."

"How did she die?"

"She committed suicide at almost the same time that I heard the moans along with the wind."

"Donnie, you creepy old goat. Forget it now ... "

"Shalini, I have ... but these things happen to me. You

have to listen to me. You have to listen to what happened this morning. No, no you have to, please. Just a few hours back, right here in this house. I had another weird experience."

"Don, I have just had a scrumptious meal of aloo ka paratha and some exotic pahari saag so please let me digest it."

It was then that Dhan Bahadur sauntered in.

"Hajoor, how is your friend's health?" he inquired in his charming Nepali Hindi.

"She is … "

"Dhan Bahadur, please sit down. I will tell you about my health."

The old man sat down on the floor, cross-legged, his eyes on the marble floor. Shalini became speechless at the sudden and uncharacteristic sharpness in my voice. She too sat down on the floor.

"Dhan Bahadur I want to tell you why I fainted," I began slowly in my best Hindi. "This morning as I was sitting right here I heard someone singing so I went out from my door into the corridor. The sound came from the second or third room from here, and there inside the room I saw a woman, a foreigner. Come I will show you where."

The old man didn't move. He kept staring at the floor while tears trickled down his wizened face like rivulets. Out of respect for his sentiments I kept quiet, feeling his sorrow flowing out of him. We didn't have to prod him. He spoke on his own, in rasping whispers.

"That is her room. She lives there. She'll always be there."

I could feel Shalini getting tense. I touched her arm, calming her.

"Who lives there?" I asked. I wanted to hear it. I wanted to be sure. So I gritted my teeth and mustered up all my courage to hear the truth while I studiously avoided Shalini.

"Rosalynn Memsaheb. She was our saheb's friend from across the seas. She was very good and very beautiful. Those days this house was filled with song and laughter and the garden too was fragrant with so many flowers. She had yellow flowers in the eastern side, pink and red in the west, white in the north and mauve in the south. She planned her garden like that. Then, one day, she discovered she was pregnant. 'Durgi' she told my wife 'he'll be a boy, as handsome as your master.' She would dance and sing but she did not tell our saheb. She knew he wouldn't like it ... but he discovered it on his own. After that there were fights every day and, one day, a doctor was brought from Shimla."

Dhan Bahadur's skeletal frame shook as he sobbed like a child. We were too stunned to respond. We could not even absorb the full import of his story. He continued, "The doctor told saheb that it was too late, he told saheb in front of Durgi ... But saheb insisted. She ... our Rosalynn memsaheb bled to death ..."

His whole body began to sway as he moaned and wept like a man in pain

"Dhan Bahadur, where's Durgi? Let me ask her to come up. Would you like some tea?" Shalini held both his shoulders and hugged him.

I dashed into the room to pack. I was shaking like a leaf. I zipped up the overnight bag and stepped back on to the verandah.

"Shalini, do let's get out of here. Let's leave him the bottle of Horlicks and the rest of the food."

"All right, let's go, he needs to be alone at such a moment."

Shalini had dismissed my morning adventure in a flash.

"Dondor, are you all right? Just take a crocin, please don't hallucinate again. Rosalynn Anne died years and years ago. Pass my wallet and let us leave him a tip. ... Here Dhan Bahadur, thank you. Relax now. We'll send Durgi up to be with you."

"She is always with me, like memsaheb. They went together, just two days apart. They both went away and left me ... "

It was then that I fled, racing down the stairs and the corridor, across the lawn without once looking back. I stopped only when I reached the half-visible road at the far corner of 'Skye End'. I saw Shalini running behind me, her face white as a sheet. I hugged her tight and made her sit down on an old tree trunk. It was then that we saw the grave with the marble slab with the words engraved on it, "Here lies Rosalynn Anne/Sweet fragrant violet/fading timelessly."

All the way to Delhi, Shalini and I held the words close to our hearts. In our own thoughts, we paid our silent tribute to a beautiful woman who had loved and lost in a house on a distant hill far away from home.

LINSINORA
THE STRANGER BY THE BROOK

The village spread like a patchwork quilt on a quiet slope overlooking the plains of Bangladesh. Small cottages with tin roofs in red, green and black sat comfortably amidst the trees with mellow autumn leaves changing into amber and rust. It was a rocky patch. Big rocks, small rocks crouched diffidently and precariously all over the hillside as if they didn't belong there. At the bottom of the western hump a brook wove its way down to the valley to join the big river on its journey to the sea. That was where she escaped every day from the monotonous predictability of her loveless home where her husband drank like there was no tomorrow and her two small children clung to their indulgent grandmother like leeches. The happy, gurgling brook at the bottom of the village was her refuge.

Every day she would rush through her daily chores with the alacrity and keenness of someone who had much to look forward to. The cleaning, tidying and cooking –

precise, mechanical, bang on time – was completed in the morning with the punctuality of an army drill. After the breakfast of red rice and stew was served and eaten, she would wash the utensils and put them out in the sun. Then, gathering the clothes to be washed, a cake of soap and a pitcher, she would head for the brook.

She would not go down the frequently used village road. She would scramble up the slope and sit on a sun-warmed rock from where she could get a spectacular view of the plains below: green villages and pools of water that sparkled in the sun like enormous jewels. Depending on the weather, and the need within, she would spend some time there.

Once her mind felt light and fresh, cleansed of the messy night and crowded morning she would begin her descent. She waited for this moment each day. Daintily she would step down the hill, smiling, as if she was meeting a long-lost lover. Every day she felt envied and special, her smile spreading on her face like sunshine on the quiet hills.

Then as she was about to reach her destination, she would slide down the hillside. She would wave her pitcher and the bundle of clothes with wild abandon, her golden skin, her ebony eyes hill-glowing, sun-sparkling, her long hair waving triumphantly in the wind.

On that particular day she had almost landed on the side of the stream when she spied someone strange sprawled on the grassy patch beside the brook, her little oasis. It was very strange indeed for it was a man she had never seen before, never, ever.

She knew, at least by face, all the young men from the neighbouring villages for they all frequented the same marketplace in a larger village close by. She knew them all, for on the Big Market Day she always set up her own stall selling not only home-grown vegetables of the season but cigarettes, bidis and tobacco brought from Shillong. They were about forty, fifty men, all jostling for her goods and attention. Apart from her own clansmen there were cousins, uncles, cousins-in-law, their friends, and, of course, her two brothers. This one was certainly not one of them. He was a stranger, and he had come uninvited to her land.

She kept the pitcher and the clothes on the ground and grabbed hold of an old stump, jagged and brittle, which pricked her mercilessly. She held on stubbornly, however, till she had lowered herself close to where the stranger was sleeping. She plucked a few wild berries and munched them thoughtfully watching him. After a while she dusted her dress and jainkyrshah of all the weeds and mud that it had collected along the flight down the hillside. Then she tiptoed a few steps closer towards the sleeping figure and stared at him.

Who was he? Where had he come from? Why was he sleeping here on this particular bend of this secluded brook, her special little domain? How did he suddenly arrive here? Was it sngi balang Wednesday? That was one of the three days in a week that the bus passed that way to bring some specially ordered goods and the post.

"Have you come to fetch water?"

All of a sudden the stranger spoke. His eyes opened and caught the lambent sunrays, startling her. Her pitcher toppled and dropped and clanked boisterously on a rock, as she ran and scrambled up the hill.

"What happened? Fill your pitcher, wash your clothes. What's the matter? Did I frighten you?"

She climbed on a rock shaped like a toadstool ringed with

pink and white daisies and glared down at him defiantly.
How dare he think I am scared? He, he – a stranger in my
land! She grabbed a stone and flung it hard in the opposite
direction. It hit a shy, totally unprepared rock with a loud
thud. She sighed, her irritation somewhat appeased by the
violence of stone on stone.

"I am not scared," she shouted in one breath and her
voice floated down like a leaf.

"Yes, I am sure you are not scared. If you are then you
insult me."

"How –what do you mean?"

"Well obviously if I scare you then there must be
something bad in me."

"Just because I am not scared of you doesn't make you
good."

"Yes, all right, but it doesn't make me bad either."

"If you are not bad then what you doing here lying on
the grass?"

"Why, do only bad people come here?"

"What a thing to say! How dare you?"

"Well that's what you are implying."

Her eyes crinkled quizzically, what on earth is he
saying? How come he seemed so relaxed, even the stone
hitting the rock did not bother him. How can a stranger
look so comfortable so far away from home? He looked
like a city slicker. His trousers were not turned up at the
bottom which meant that they were neither hand-me-
downs or bought at the shop which blatantly sold second
hand foreign clothes meant for charity. His shoes were
neither dirty nor old and tattered.

"Whatever it is, what are you doing here?"

"Why are you so worried? How much privacy do you need to wash your clothes? Am I intruding?"

"Yes, of course you are. No stranger has ever come here to just sleep around like this!"

"There's always a first time for everything, you know."

"What?"

"Oh! Never mind. Basically you want to know why I am here, right?"

"Well naturally," she said, flicking the rebellious strands of her hair from her face with an imperious wave. She looked straight into his eyes, waiting for an answer, straining her ears against the passing wind.

"See, I have come from Shillong and I was going to visit a cousin in Laitlum the next village … "

"I know where it is!"

"All right … well as I was passing by in the bus, I saw this clean brook gurgling away happily. After a long, long time I had this most uplifting feeling within me. The brook reminded me of an innocent baby and I wanted to spend some time next to it, just to absorb some of the …well … vibrations. I seek places like these. I write songs you know and I get inspiration from such places. I told the driver to stop the bus and I got off. That's all."

"You are crazy!"

"Am I?"

"Of course you are! You are definitely crazy!"

She scrambled up the hill and half hid behind a lantana bush and kept observing him. Her eyes didn't leave him for a minute.

"You are crazy!"

"I don't think I am crazy. I think people who don't get moved by such delightful sights are crazy. They are pathetic! They are living in hell."

"Hell? How dare you? What do you mean?"

"Hell my dear is an empty heart. Try to feel..."

"WHAT are we supposed to feel?"

"Don't you know? Don't you feel anything when you come here?"

"No" she spat out defiantly. In that one single moment she realized that, indeed, she came there every day because she felt something else, somewhere else, strangely safe and special. Disturbed by her own discovery and her dishonesty she turned her face away, her perfect profile silhouetted against the azure sky.

"No?"

She heard his question but did not answer. She hugged herself tight trying to contain herself and then quickly took refuge in her mind. She felt kind of displaced by this intrusion both in her physical and mental space. She decided that it was indeed a very unusual afternoon. So she arranged her clothes and other belongings on the ground and sat still with her chin on her knees.

What a strange man! Her husband wouldn't think like that would he? She had never heard him say. "What beautiful sunshine," not even on golden January mornings, so special and so welcomed, for usually it was grey and sunless. By the time he got up from his drunken slumber the sun would have moved to the backyard where the chicken coop and pigsty sat close to each other in a corner. He would sip his tea sullenly not speaking, covered from head to foot in an old grey and maroon tapmohkhlieh. Later he would stroll down to the marketplace to smoke a pipe with his cronies. If he managed to get some work loading and unloading goods from trucks and buses he would bring home some food, some meat if he had earned enough or just dried fish and chillies. Otherwise, he would tumble in late in the evening, after the children had gone to sleep, bringing in only his fatigue and frustration, and go to bed. Sometimes in the middle of the night he would mumble and fumble and make advances towards her. She shivered with remembered repulsion as her eyes travelled down to the stranger below.

He was lying in a splash of afternoon light as the sky changed colour into a lighter blue preparing for sunset and the ebbing away of yet another day. He had crossed his feet and his hands were behind his head supporting and cushioning it like a pillow. His eyes seemed half closed. She wasn't sure. So she slipped down a little and craned her neck to see. The wind had tousled his hair this way and that way, very dark brown hair. Strange hair, she thought.

"You know your hair is the colour of cowdung," she shouted, smirking, provoking him, feeling very satisfied with her daring. Somehow she desperately wanted to know him, to chat with him and hear things she had not heard before.

"Really?"

"Yes."

She looked carefully at his face for some sign of irritation and discomfort. That was how she knew men. She would feel so much more at ease if this stranger were to behave predictably. Her stepfather and husband were always in some kind of angry flap and they were the only men she really knew in all her twenty years. She tried again.

"How come you have this funny coloured hair? Khasis have black hair."

"Well, this cowdung mop is thanks to my great-grandfather. He was a Brit."

"A what?"

"A saheb. A man from England, Scotland. God alone knows where."

"Where? From Bilat?"

"Ah! Yes, so you know".

"Of course, I know. What do you think? All white men come from Bilat."

"Hmn … "

"What was his name?"

"God knows … "

"Surely, so do you?"

"No. How does it matter?"

"Yes, I suppose it doesn't matter, as long as God knows," she sighed, feeling rather erudite and important that at last she found something she could agree on with the stranger. "He must have been one of those soldiers passing through during that big war long ago. Do you have a photograph? Imagine your grandmother didn't even get a chance to wear a veil and all that!"

"No, I don't think so. Who wastes time and money on veils and stuff anyway?" he laughed.

"What's so funny huh? I wore a veil. My cousin presented it to me. She brought it all the way from Bangladesh."

"Smuggled it."

"What? What does that mean?"

"Oh! nothing. So you are married."

"Yes".

"What is your name?"

"Linsinora."

"What a grand name! Lin-si-no-ra!"

"Are you making fun again?"

"Of course not! Do you have children?"

"Yes, two."

"What does your husband do?"

"What do you do?"

"I compose songs and I play the drums in a band."

"Oh! That's what most people do in Shillong isn't it? Anyway good for you! Well my husband...."

She stretched out on the warm slope and put her hands behind her head just like the stranger and stared dreamily at the quiet slope in front.

"My husband is such a wonderful man, a very good man. He works very hard in the fields all day. We grow potatoes and maize. At midday I walk across with his meal of rice and meat. In the morning you see, he doesn't get time to eat except for a cup of tea and a small plate of rice and salt, sometimes an ata or two. We sit amidst the fields of crops and chat while he eats. Sometimes I take the children too. It's so refreshing out there in the fields. After he has finished his meal and had his smoke I walk back, plucking wild herbs on the way like jamyrdoh, jatira, pudina, jaiur according to the season. My husband works so hard. He really does. At dusk when he returns he washes his hands and feet and then I press his body for at least half an hour till all his tiredness dissipates. He works so hard, my husband, really hard. And he doesn't even drink – not a drop – ever! By next year we'll have enough money to add an extra room. I would like it next to the kitchen. The window will look out onto our vegetable garden. When the mustard flowers bloom it'll look like a carpet of gold.

What a feast for the eyes! You'd never see a sight like that in the city, would you? I have never been to Shillong. Is it very much bigger than Nongstoin? Is it?"

There was no response so she stirred and looked. She didn't realize that her eyes were heavy with sleep as she lay down on the sun warmed earth. She shook her head and rubbed her eyes, once, twice, three times, but there was no mistake. The stranger was gone. Her eyes, her heart, her soul searched high and low all over the hills, down in the valley as the sky turned into a dreamy pink and the brook a misty grey flecked with the memories of the day gone by. But he was gone.

"How could you? How could you?" she cried out. "How could you go away just like that?"

She wept and wept. She wept for that one glorious moment and also for its passing. Then slowly she got up and gathered her belongings. Her clothes were unwashed, her work undone. She smiled. She knew that that day would stay with her forever in her heart and, sometimes, she could escape into it too and seek shelter in its strange and special space. Filled with gratitude she sang a favourite childhood ditty ... and made her way back to the village.

In the distance a bus droned away and disappeared in a cloud of dust. Inside the bus a man was writing a song.

DALINIA
MEMORIES OF A LOVE UNTOLD

For a long, long time Dalinia had no memory of that summer ... until one November morning at the Shillong Golf Course.

On that fine, blue-skied morning the town's golfing fraternity had gathered for the inauguration of a glamorous national level tournament: there were the big shots from the bureaucracy, the armed forces, the police, the business community, the media and the colourful local gentry in their tweeds and suede shoes and charming accents. Dalinia's husband, a senior IAS officer and a golf enthusiast, had been looking forward to the event and along with Dalinia, he reached the golf course well ahead of time. "We must go and see that everything is in order. After all, people from all over India are arriving, everything should be tiptop. Imagine Da, even Farooq Abdullah is expected! What an honour! How I wish Kapil Dev had not backed out," Bantei had said that morning, his excitement bristling through the house.

Bantei Roy's most charming quality was his positive energy, his enthusiasm for all the activities that made up his well planned life. His confidence stemmed from the respect he got from his colleagues, being one of the few to have made it to the services on the merit list, no quota. Sometimes at a party, however, when an officer from mainland India went over the top with that 'special treatment', Bantei and Dalinia would look at each other a little embarrassed, knowing that the others in the room were fully aware of what was going on and were not feeling good about it. Deep inside they wished people would look beyond position and wealth like it was in the world they grew up in.

Dalinia had chewed the last bite of her scrambled eggs on toast and nodded 'hmn'. She couldn't speak for her mouth was full and she silently thanked God for small mercies. Dalinia Dkhar belonged to an old, conservative family that considered golf a sport for the westernized and frowned-upon crowd in spite of the fact that many members of her family had availed of the best education in the West. After she married Bantei Roy (Ban to his friends), an Edmundian with half-British grandparents on both sides, she was sucked into a world different and distant to the one she grew up in. Here, her education helped – Pine Mount School, Shillong, Indraprastha College, Delhi – all that certainly helped as the beautiful wife of the young and handsome ADM (Assistant District Magistrate) when she partied with his colleagues from all over India. And, of course, when she entertained at home and the fridge was emptied of all the beef delicacies and pork too – depending on who was dining with them on that particular evening.

Otherwise she thrived on her job as a lecturer in a local college, her two beautiful children and her orderly home that formed the foundation of her life. She poured all the knowledge she had imbibed in her History classes in Delhi into her work with the kind of fervor and diligence that the college had not seen in decades. Her colleagues, who were all extremely fond of her, however, noticed that she studiously avoided talking of anything other than making small talk and discussing her subject. At home, one day, something happened which could have given the family an inkling of another side of Dalinia, but the incident passed unnoticed. Her elder daughter had come back from school filled with excitement about a new girl from the tea gardens who had joined school that day. "Oh Mei! We have a new girl in class – Lin Brooks … " Dalinia who was putting some tiger lilies in a vase gasped and the vase fell and broke. "What happened Mei? Wait, I will get a broom – I will call the maid – wait – Linda Brooks is so friendly and pretty. She has been chosen for the basketball team. Such fun! Here comes the broom and dough!" The pieces of glass were carefully removed with wet dough. It was pressed all over the carpet and the floor so as to collect every tiny piece of broken glass. After this the area was carefully broomed. Along with the pieces of broken glass the entire incident was simply swept away and forgotten.

On that particular November morning, since it was not just any golf tournament but a national level one, Dalinia dressed with great care. To match her muka jainsem with a maroon border she wore the traditional string of coral beads with matching earrings and ring, maroon shoes and a ryndia stem falling neatly down from her left shoulder. She was representing her community and she was going to give it her best shot. She knew that being tribal meant she always had to work doubly hard to be accepted as 'okay', 'good', maybe 'very good' in whatever she did in the bureaucratic world peopled with so many from beyond the hills. This was one aspect in her life that she was never in doubt of and which she shared with her husband. It transcended all barriers and differences in background and upbringing. It was the single most important unifying and enriching factor in her marriage to Bantei. They must always give their best.

So, although Dalinia was not really interested in golf, that morning she saw herself gazing at the century old club with pride. Captain Jackson and C. R. Rhodes had developed the club and the course in 1889. The course spread out like a carpet from the club, most of its eighteen holes nestled amidst the tall pines in the distance. Her father-in-law had once told her that there was a time when a nine-hole course existed in the area around the Garrison Ground, Civil Hospital, Lady Hydari Park and her school, Pine Mount. She remembered all this as she observed the people pouring in, on that fine November morning, in the Shillong Golf Course.

It was then that, all of a sudden, she saw someone very familiar framing the main entrance of the club. Nattily dressed in quiet colours he stood out because of his height and perfect Aryan features. Dalinia froze. She would have most certainly collapsed if Barilin had not been holding her arm albeit for a different reason. "Isn't that man handsome? Whew! What great looks! I hope he wins, no?" she gushed as she squeezed Dalinia's arm excitedly. Dalinia simply stared, as her head swam, reeling back to distant memories when she was a young girl in a city far away.

"Who's he Bari?" Dalinia managed to ask after what seemed like a lifetime. Bari, loud and daring with her plunging necklines and three broken marriages, was actually no friend of hers, but at that moment she was the only one who shared a special moment.

"Arjun Kapur from Cal," Barilang whispered back.

Arjun. Arjun. Dalinia searched her mind, journeying deep into the forgotten corridors of her memory. She had heard this name before; of course she had, "I have a younger brother who is still in school. His name is Arjun. There are two sisters in between." She could hear the words, the voice floating along with the mist from a heart-wrenching moment long ago. She wriggled out of Bari's grasp with great effort, tossed her hair as she always did when she needed confidence and taking a deep breath, glided to her husband. "Bantei, I am not feeling well. I will go and rest for a while. I will just be back." Before her husband could respond she walked away quickly to the car park.

The driver was nowhere to be seen. He had obviously, not expected to be back on duty so soon. His buddy, the club barman, had informed him that there would be lunch and tea as well with plenty of liquor before, after and in between. So he had made his own plans confidently. He had his own dreams that November morning. Dalinia leant against her white Ambassador, the official car, her head swimming all over again. Just down the road in a small tea shop Bah Rit, the driver was snuggling upto the voluptuous Letsi. People kept coming to buy provisions – kwai, cigarettes, bidis, toffees, biscuits, nimkis (called muthrees in the north) and, of course, tea and soft drinks totally unaware of what was going on behind the counter. The more observant presumed that Letsi's unusually red cheeks and shining eyes were due to the crisp wind and the sunshine that brightened up her little shop.

Dalinia steadied her nerves and was about to return to the course when she spied the Deputy Commissioner's driver strolling into the car park.

"Have you seen my driver?" she asked frantically.

"No, madam. Should I go and look for him? Do you want to go somewhere madam?"

"Yes. I have to rush off to Cleeve Colony. My cousin is not well. She just called me" Dalinia lied, biting her lip sheepishly.

"Madam, I can drop you. I have plenty of time before I pick up sir's children from the school," he assured her.

Once Dalinia got into the car, so overwhelmed was she with relief that she quite forgot that what she was doing was far from correct. She slid down in her seat a little, just enough to relax, but not deep enough for passersby to later comment that Kong Dalinia was sleeping in an official car at ten o'clock in the morning, that Kong Dalinia was not by her husband's side during that important event in the golf course. As the car climbed up to Cleeve Colony she felt the pine scented air caress her face. She opened her eyes and directed the driver to her cousin's house, Shaikordor Dkhar, who she found soaking in the sun with a college friend, visiting from Australia.

"What story?" Shai said genuinely puzzled and added, "And why are you looking so pale and what happened to the golf tournament? You are supposed to be there!"

"It's all connected and please, if you don't mind ... just let me speak," Dalinia replied. "I need to."

"Yes, just let her relax, Shai, let us not stress her further. Just talk it out you'll feel much better. I'd love to hear a story … is it a love story? Yes? I don't believe this. Tell, tell me, tell me. An Indian love story, what a treat!" Avril Cooper said gently. She didn't quite know what the fuss was all about and what she was about to hear but realized that she was in the midst of an unusual situation.

"A what story?" Shaikordor, secretly referred to as "the confirmed spinster", looked as if she was about to faint when she realized that even if she did, it wouldn't make a difference. Dalinia was reclining on the easy chair and her eyes were far away. Nevertheless she couldn't contain herself from expressing her shock, completely rattled, she shouted, "Da! What on earth…"

"Come Shai, let your cousin be. Da, relax and just talk … Take your time, Da, it's all right," Avril said, while cousin Shai stared, not knowing what to say.

So Dalinia talked. She told her story. A story that had crouched so far inside her memory it had almost lost its way back.

1

I met him fourteen years ago when I was in college in Delhi University and Saihunlang was in Woodstock, Mussoorie.

I was nineteen and Saihun was fifteen. That summer Mei and Pa had decided to rent a cottage near her school to spend the usual few weeks' break in the summer.

They had admitted her in Woodstock School because she was keen to do her college in the US. Every so often, however, they would fret and worry because she was so far away from Shillong and in an alien place, yet they had no choice. Sai was brilliant and determined – hence the summer plan was made, much to my delight.

I was longing to be with Saihun because our holidays clashed and I was seeing too little of my vivacious little sister. Besides ... besides I was strangely drawn to the northern mountains ever since I visited the Kumaon hills during a college trip in my first year.

I'd dream of those snow-topped mountains and long for the day when I'd experience the famous bewitching, enchanting mist that my friends had talked so much about. And believe me, in Mussoorie the mist didn't let me down. It was late summer when the monsoon arrived. It was also the season of the mist.

It would wait outside the cottage when I woke up every morning and taking me gently in its arms – that's how I felt – the mist would guide me all day into a world wrapped in dreams.

Completely enchanted by the hill town, my nineteen-year-old heart waited tremulously for love.

You know, Mussoorie was discovered in 1827 by Captain Young, a commandant of the 1st Gurkhas of the Sirmur Rifles based in Dehra Dun. One day while he was out hunting he strayed up the slopes and on reaching the top, was so exhilarated by the cool mountain air that he immediately set up a sanatorium for convalescing officers and named the little township Landour, after Llandowror, a town in South Wales. On a hill top he built his residence, Mullingar Hill. I learnt about these details later – when ... you will discover that soon, as I go along.

As I passed it that morning I inhaled it deeply, the crisp fresh air, as Captain Young must have done, almost a hundred and fifty years ago, relieved, comforted, inspired.

Colourful prayer flags fluttered in the wind, the house and the surrounding area was now a Tibetan settlement.

The neighbouring village of Mansuri also developed along with Landour into one of the most beautiful hill stations in North India where the Indian royalty and the Indian elite spent many long and languid summers. To many, Mussoorie was considered more beautiful than Shimla and Nainital. Not anymore though – crowded and unplanned, it has lost its charm.

In Landour's Char Dukan the air had not changed since the days of Captain Young. It was still so fresh and fragrant like so many perennials that sustain us and rein us in through the many whirlwinds that sweep into our lives. I would pass this picturesque oasis every day during my walks.

It was the last day of our stay and I shall call this part of the story the Morning of the Mist. We were leaving the following afternoon and I had prayed all night that before leaving I would not be deprived of a mist-filled morning. I prayed hard like I used to as a child for a much longed – for Christmas present.

I woke up early, tiptoed out of bed and with bated breath drew the curtain. I will never forget that moment. It was like … like a divine revelation! Everything outside, the cottages tumbling down the slopes, the trees, tall firs, spread-eagled pines, frizzy poplars, the tiny mountain daisies, pink-cheeked school children, hill-folk in their caps and puffing pipes … they all seemed to be floating in that sea of mist.

I stepped out of the cottage and climbed up to the knoll just above it and sat there huddled up, savouring the touch of the swirling mist. It was very, very quiet, there were no birds in the trees, no breeze blowing through, just the vast expanse of the white sky above and the valley below. It must have been like that at the beginning of Time.

It was so quiet but deep inside I felt I was not alone. Deep inside my heart longed to reach out to the vastness beyond – to what and to whom I couldn't tell.

I don't know how long I sat there before my ears picked up a sound in the distance, the sound of brisk footsteps. Tak! Tak! Tak! Tak! As the minutes ticked away the sound became louder and louder, closer and closer, louder and closer, closer and louder and then, all at once – silence. The landscape, pale and sunless, continued to blur more and more as the mist rose from the gorge below, wandering like a lost, disintegrated ghost. Parts of it embraced the trees, caressed the cottages and held me tenderly in its vulnerable world. That's how I felt.

"What more could anyone ever want?" I whispered to the mist, hugging myself happily and I heard a voice reply, "How right you are! For once, someone is saying something right." I turned to meet a pair of light brown eyes set in a startlingly good-looking face of perfect Aryan features. The face ... it was ... red with the whip of the morning wind and glowing with the wisdom of many lives. Before I could say a word, however, the man had walked away, disappearing quickly into the encircling grey.

That was our first meeting.

2

The second time we met, was on the night of the Giant Wheel. In those days in the late '70s there were fairly large empty, grassy spaces in the middle of Connaught Place.

Every now and then they would come alive with the colour and bustle of a mela. That year, four of us friends from college decided to attend it. I was very excited. I had never been to a mela in Delhi.

From the description given by my friends, however, I had presumed it would be something like the iew in the village of Smit, a delightful extension of the Shad Nongkrem, a five-day festival held by the royal family and the subjects of the Hima of Nongkrem. Avril, it is something you have to experience.

The iew stretches for miles on the meadows beyond the chieftain's residence, the iing sad. There are mouth-watering local delicacies to suit all palates, exotic fruits and rice cakes, trinkets and toys, cane baskets and mats, locally made knives, swords, axes, spades and other unique implements and, of course, the much-awaited and generously-consumed rice beer. There was always a lot of gaiety as the village belles flirted and ran from stall to stall followed by young, eager yokels. Many a heart was broken and mended, many marriage alliances were suggested and finalized. It was such fun watching it all, eating our putharo and pudoh in a smoky tea stall. In front of the iing sad, however, the scene was solemn and regal as the princes and princesses, along with participants from all over the hima and the Khasi Hills, danced to the traditional beat of the pipes and drums. After the dance was over and the goats were sacrificed, in the moonlit frontyard of his palace, the chieftain would dance, his sword flashing, his yak tail whisk catching the falling moonbeams and stardust. On the rolling meadows beyond, the bamboo torches were lit, transforming the entire place into Camelot. That was my idea of a fair, a mela.

You must simply experience it one day, Avril. In fact, you have just missed it. It is always held in the first week of this month, November. I described it to my friends on that day long ago, still so steeped in my own world back home.

"It's something like that, Da." Urvashi, my room-mate had laughed. "Plenty of fun and games and trinkets to buy but none of that culture vulture bit!" I was excited all the same, as I always was with something new in the different world that I'd been flung into. A period in my life which I will never regret. It expanded my horizons. It helped me grow and understand about life beyond the hills ... about life itself.

It started off very well, the evening, just four of us all set for the mela. There was no tension about dressing up and hoping that the boy each one of us had a crush on would reciprocate appropriately. Those days were different and a girl couldn't chase a boy openly. All we could do was dress up as attractively as possible which meant flowers in our hair, extra kaajal in our eyes and dollops of coyness and modesty with just about enough humour and laughter to attract attention and impress ... or so we thought.

We were straight out of convents and sheltered homes where we had soaked in the teachings of well-meaning nuns and elders. Besides, being from the Northeast I was extra careful not to be too loud either in dress or behaviour. These instructions had been given in an hour-long lecture by one of my aunts, before I joined Delhi University. Nah Sela was married to a Punjabi and lived in Ludhiana. I did not quite understand her grim determination to convince me "everywhere it's the same Da, everyone is doing the same thing but here they are discreet. We are too open and blatant ... especially the women of some of the other tribes, so we get a bad name. I feel bad saying all this but I feel I should. One has to be extra careful otherwise you will get harassed. You will get a bad name."

Yeah, I didn't quite get what she meant. I quietly replied that I didn't quite understand what she was talking about. Back home I knew very few girls who were sleeping around and I didn't think any of my friends in Delhi were either. "Be discreet in your dress, speech and behaviour," she continued regardless, and flounced out of the room.

Those days we never questioned elders and we were so innocent! Besides I was so reserved and had just arrived in Delhi and I actually thought she was batty. Later, on those trips to Connaught Place and South Extension when we would get pinched and pawed and we would encounter men who exposed themselves, I understood. Terrified, I never took a bus in Delhi and would avoid short cuts and lonely alleys.

Coming back to my story ... all those preparations almost every weekend, the decking up bit needed both time and effort and we were grateful that on that Saturday evening we could bond and chill and be ourselves and merry without that awful thought "I hope she is not looking better than me."

I must admit here though that after the Morning of the Mist I had ceased to care. I felt complete and connected as if my search was over.

Nothing was as delicious as the memory and ... the hope.

Urvashi, Arti, Sushma and I had a ball at the mela. We played all the games, sampled all the delicacies, bought hair-clips, bangles, earrings, nose rings, toe rings, bindis, necklaces and wore every single one of them ... giggling and collapsing with laughter. We were merry in our innocence and our youth. ... We kept the ride on the giant wheel for the very end. We sat in front of the 'Photo Tent' waiting for our turn. We had to wait for a group of four to disembark because all four of us wanted to ride together.

The Photo Tent was to me, more startling than everything else around. Well, there was this tent and inside it stood a life-sized doll scantily dressed with blonde hair, blue eyes in a provocative pose. Boys and men were lining up to take photos cuddling up to this doll! Urvashi said to me, "They don't get this far in real life so it's damn good for them. Hah! And she's blonde and blue-eyed so these buggers don't get guilty pangs mid-way. You know ... Oh God! It's not my sister is it?"

I just stared at Urvashi. She always came out with these startling statements I didn't know what to say or think but I felt kind of sad.

North India was so different from the rest of the country in those days. Girls could not get too friendly with the opposite sex. If one did, she was considered 'fast' and a tart except for a certain group in college who had gatherings where they had musical evenings with rock and jazz and smoked a lot of hash, boys and girls mixed freely and danced and dated without fear and guilt. Most of these kids came from educated and westernized homes with dads in either the creative or the corporate world and some were from old business houses.

All that hit me hard when I first arrived in this world so full of strange values and opinions on everything – "all hype and hypocrisy" Urvashi said. I was kind of stuck in between. I guess that was why I decided to dream instead and hoped that my dreams would turn to reality.

This was almost half a century ago of course. Things have changed a lot since then. I keep asking about this but no one seems to be sure. "All the women still get harassed and worse – not only Northeasterners. How would a North Indian guy sleep in peace unless he has belittled at least one female?" Stuff like that is the usual reply ... Not that I cared, for me it had become just another space with a name ... till today.

Aunt Sela's words would come back to me every now and again as I went through unpleasant experiences. I remember my Sikkimese friend, Sonam, fainted when she was hitching a ride and as she was getting into the front seat she noticed that the well dressed man at the wheel had a huge bulge inside his trousers which he was casually pulling out. If Urvashi was there she would have hit him cold with her umbrella. We fled. I puked and Sush and Arti sobbed as they dragged Sonam out and revived her. Days later we laughed our guts out. It made us feel better. I became more grateful for Nah Sela's visit all the way from Ludhiana, wondering what she must be going through.

Yet this story is about disobedience. How I strayed and loved and lived and danced – though for just awhile, just for awhile.

I keep digressing but Delhi and all these strange experiences are coming back to me and Mussoorie with all its magic is so much part of my story or maybe I am going slow, savouring each word like a sip of cognac.

To get back to the mela ... the giant wheel was a multi-coloured monstrosity which rocked and rolled to Hindi pop. Arti, Sushma and Urvashi sang gustily along with the rest of the crowd. Urvashi, of course, had had a few drags of hash before we came and was in top form. Up we swung as the mela flashed by below in all its fluorescence. Down we dropped and then up again. For a split second while perched on top one could get a glimpse of the shops and restaurants of C.P and the cars whizzing by. This continued for quite a while before my eyes began to wander all over the man-conceived fairyland.

It was then that I saw him leaning against an ice cream stand, brown eyes smiling, his dark brown curly mop tousled by the wind. I waved and smiled, my heart racing and pounding and remembering ... the Morning of the Mountain Mist. He waved back too and smiled... I waved again and he waved back as the giant wheel tossed me up for the last lap of the ride

As soon as I got off I ran, weaving through the crowd, looking for the ice cream stand. I found it; I couldn't miss it because it had a Zeenat Aman poster pasted in front and "Dum Maro Dum" written coquettishly below it. I found it but he wasn't there. I stared at the stand and it stared back forlornly, as a passing wind brushed passed me, whispering its apologies.

Tears fell from my eyes and ran down my face. "Don't cry beautiful one. Come let's just share a joint," a long-haired hippie said, sidling up to me.

"No, thanks" I replied though I desperately searched his face in case he had a clue and an explanation. But his face was blank.

He, too, was waiting for an answer.

3

That night I tossed and turned till, finally, unable to control my bewilderment and sorrow I woke up Urvashi.

I told her everything. I don't know how much she heard, she was sleepy and tired and I took my time telling the story. I couldn't race through it. In fact, unconsciously, I was relishing each word, reliving each moment as I am now. At the end, when I was silent Urvashi sprang up like a jack-in-the-box. "DALINIA, for God's sake, get yourself a boyfriend! Your obsession with Alain Delon has got to END! You are hallucinating. Nakul Narayan adores you and he's smart and ... please Da, let's get some sleep. Good night."

I stared at her as she turned away and went back to sleep. Inside me I could feel everything collapsing, dissolving. I felt so alone and empty. Finally, when my tears had dried and I was drained and had nothing left inside, I slept.

Next day Urvashi and Arti and Sushma sat me down and talked to me in quiet tones, as if I was a basket case. At the movies the following weekend I found myself sitting next to Nakul Narayan and, afterwards, at the dinner in Geeti's Greater Kailash house, Uday Singh and Rahul Trehan were attentiveness personified under the watchful eyes of my girlfriends. We were all sipping some gin and lime which was the college girl drink of those days – two small pegs – and feeling grown up and sophisticated! Sure I felt good, I was dreaming all the time!

Back in the hostel on Sunday evening my three friends sulked; their plans had not worked. They were worried, irritated and Urvashi was, true to her nature, insulted. For a whole week we studiously avoided the topic.

Life continued normally in college as the winter gave way to yet another spring.

Eight weeks after the Night of the Giant wheel Urvashi had to eat her words. I met him again, my first real meeting like any other couple, at Urvashi's parents' place. It was the occasion of her brother's marriage in Mumbai.

I call that moment in time the Evening of the Rising Sea

4

The wedding fell on a Wednesday and was preceded by Holi on the Monday. So the hostel warden was magnanimous enough to grant us six nights-out in a row after we vowed that we would forfeit our outings for the rest of the term and, more importantly, after Urvashi had presented her with a cream and maroon silk saree and a bottle of cologne. "Since you can't come to Bombay, Ma'am my parents have sent you this small gift," Urvashi explained, faking coyness and timidity which didn't suit her at all, but the ploy worked. The saree was a new, unworn one of Sushma's and 'Topaz' an unused birthday present of mine. Later in, Bombay Sushma and I were duly compensated.

It was the night of Anil's bachelor party. Since the wedding was to be held at a hotel it was decided that the big bash would be held at home. The parents left for Lonavla. They went to spend two nights on their own in order to relax and unwind before the big event. So the sixth floor where the parents lived was all ours and the seventh, the floor Anil had done up for himself and his bride was where the party was to be held.

The sea was, to me, an absolute delight. In the mornings I would watch the fishing boats silhouetted against the sky on its calm waters. When the sunlight streamed down, the water sparkled and children jumped and frolicked in the sand. As party time was drawing near, the sky blushed a deep, warm pink in the distance as the red sun slowly sank into a sea of clouds. Then, gradually, with the changing colours of the sky, the waves turned volatile, leaping like angry warriors – the waves, those waves – I will never forget – for it was against the backdrop of those waves that I met him. That is why I call it the Evening of the Rising Sea.

Everything that happens, good or bad, in life is pre-destined. It just happens, you cannot prevent it. I believe in that and that is how I cope.

As it happened I was watching the changing face of the sea, totally mesmerized, when Urvashi walked in with a tall and handsome young man.

"Dalinia, meet ... "

"Alain Delon ... " I finished off for her, pronouncing the words in a special way, feeling spunky all of a sudden.

Urvashi eyes saucered and so did his and all three of us collapsed with laughter for different reasons.

"Hi! Well, it's not Alain but Ashwin, not Delon but just plain simple Kapur. Sad isn't it?" he said, his eyes twinkling "Maybe that's why I took so long to introduce myself."

"What?" Urvashi looked genuinely perplexed.

"We've met twice before – once in Mussoorie for five minutes and then, a few weeks ago in a mela in Delhi we saw each other. Am I right Dalinia?"

Urvashi fled. I smiled and my heart opened and embraced that moment tenderly.

After that everything just fell into place. We lived each moment with such intensity that it hurt and yet there was no other way we could have lived. During the wedding celebrations we were inseparable: throughout the dance and music, the wine and food, the pulsating gaiety. I don't, to this day, remember what I wore and what I ate and drank, but I remember, very distinctly that I was floating in absolute bliss, at that immensely happy occasion.

"What joy! How long does it last?" I heard myself whisper to the not-so-distant sea and he replied, "As long as one can still imagine." I laughed and he laughed and we walked hand in hand to the dance floor and waltzed to 'Lara's Theme.' Before I slept I thought – what a strange answer – as long as one can still imagine.

Is love imaginary? Is it true then that everything is but an illusion? In the distance a roar of an answer seemed to come with the tide but before I could decode it I was fast asleep.

Namita and Anil looked so comfortable together greeting the guests, talking and laughing. Theirs was an arranged marriage and they had met five or six times, without a chaperone, before they were wed. "Their families have a common friend who arranged the match, Dalinia. That is half the battle won; fewer adjustment problems. That's like knowing each other well."

"Which means I don't know you at all Ash?" I asked. He looked straight into my eyes and said, "We've known each other through many lives." That happened on my last day by the sea. Then he led me to the verandah and said, "The song of the sea doesn't end at the shore but in the hearts of those who listen to it."

"Gibran..." I said. I smiled. He didn't, his eyes on the waves, merging, withdrawing, merging, withdrawing.

I watched, fascinated but I asked for no explanations for you only question when you are sad.

5

The middle of our story I call The Days of Star Spangled Delights. He had moved from his home-town Kolkata to a barsati in Defence Colony which is, perhaps, the most centrally situated up-market colony in Delhi. He was working on his second book, quite different from the one he wrote soon after his Oxford years, which was a work of pure fiction. This one was tentatively entitled 'How Many Parents Are Fit to Be Parents?'. He wanted to research in Delhi, a city he felt was in urgent need of help. "In twenty years there will be a terribly disturbed generation unless parents realize and accept that parenting is the most serious of all career options." Frankly, I couldn't quite understand that what he visualized would in fact be relevant in places like Shillong, Aizawl, Dimapur, Imphal, Guwahati – just about everywhere. I just gazed admiringly at him as he talked.

Like him, whatever he said came from a different world – remote, exciting and exclusive.

Every day we would talk on the phone late at night because the college phone booth was always busy till 10 p.m. There were no cell phones then and even girls from affluent homes had to line up to call. It was so exciting that long wait while I rehearsed over and over again what I was going say, choosing the words carefully, to match his flawless English.

The weekends were blissful. I would go over to his barsati and tidy it up as much as possible without him noticing while he was in the bathroom or talking on the phone. He didn't like me shuffling around while he was in the room just as much as I – a true blue Northeasterner –

did not approve of messy homes. He was always thinking except when we were cooking, chatting, and singing Bob Dylan, Cat Stevens and Carole King. The making love bit took a long time to come! It was like that those days ... At first I would, in fact, go over with my friends who would stay for a decent interval over cokes or coffee before they left. The two of us would then chat for hours, holding hands before we would walk down either to Akasaka or Chunghwa for Chinese food and a movie afterwards. He wasn't much of a disco person but for my sake he would escort me to the Cellar and the Wheels where we drank beer and ate sliced pork with rice and danced to Santana, Diana Ross and Mick Jagger. He was very sporting. By midnight he would drop me to my local guardian on Barakhamba Road. Sunday we met after lunch and we would go to Bengali Market for tea and walk in the grounds around India Gate before I took an auto to college twenty minutes away (in those days). He would drive off in an old Fiat borrowed from an uncle for his stay in Delhi, waving sadly because I wouldn't let him drop me to college. "Ash you are from a different world. Back in college it would be shocking if boyfriends start dropping their girlfriends so openly."

That was Delhi University in the '70s when a lot of things still hid inside one's head.

6

With May came the college summer break and I travelled to Guwahati in the Assam Mail. The summer evoked strange longings and new emotions within me. I was sleeping one afternoon on a shaded slope in Barapani after a heavy picnic lunch when I dreamt that I was back in Delhi and I was racing towards him on an empty road with neon lights winking on either side. Just when I was about to reach him and fall into his arms I woke up. I remember feeling the most excruciating pain in the pit of my stomach and a huge lump in my throat as I tried to control my tears so that my cousins wouldn't notice.

That night I rang him up and told him about the dream. He said, "Da, today it's exactly a year since we first met and sweetheart it's like a special birthday and I love you." I started crying, "How can I forget! What is wrong with me ... tell me, Ash, tell me? And on such a day how can we be so far apart? This is not fair, not fair!" Silly me – I started to cry. It was not only what he revealed to me that overwhelmed me, it was the way he recited Richard Bach, his voice breaking through the miles on seagull wings.

I cannot go to be with you
because I am already there.
You are not little because you are
already grown, playing among your
lifetimes as do we all, for
the fun of living.

You have no birthday
because you have always lived;
you were never born. And never will you die
You are not the child of the people
you call mother and father, but
their fellow-adventurer on a
bright journey to understand
the things that are.

Fly free and happy beyond
birthdays and across forever,
and we'll meet now and then when we wish,
in the midst of the one celebration
that can never end.

"Dalinia, there's no such place as far away."

Soon after, I bought this exquisite piece of literature by Richard Bach. I had to go down all the way to Guwahati to get it ... and I learnt it by heart. Thus the summer passed in Shillong – hectic and rain-swept but deep inside I was calm, I was happy and I was content.

For, at last, I needed "neither ring nor bird to fly alone above the quiet clouds."

7

I flew back to Delhi on the 10th of July. Trains were delayed and plying erratically because of the monsoon. I was a week early for college. I had planned it that way. I wanted a whole undisturbed week with Ashwin. It wasn't difficult convincing my parents because Arti's birthday fell on the 5th and that was as good an excuse as any. "Just go home and relax Da, we'll be back in Delhi by the 14th," she told me over the telephone from Bangalore, where she had gone to drop her younger sister to school, along with her parents.

I reached Arti's flat, after a delayed flight, which bumped frighteningly over Bangladesh (then East Pakistan) and east UP. I had a long shower and changed into a caftan, then I called Ash and said, "I am here in Delhi. Surprised? Yes, I came early because I want to go and see the mist in Mussoorie."

"Da, I'd love too. I'd simply love to. When do we leave?"

"Tonight by the Doon–Mussoorie Express."

That journey through the night was something I treasured for many, many years knowing, somehow, that it would be a once-in-a-lifetime experience. The most exquisite moments were of watching him sleep, as the train pierced through the night, its long whistle heralding the approaching of a stop, the end of someone's journey, the beginning of someone else's: endings and beginnings meeting like old souls but for a while. "Is this what life is all about?" I asked the Spirits of the Night. There was no answer to my question because there wasn't one. Perhaps what I had asked was not a question but an answer.

It was the answer to all questions… only there were several ways of wording it.

The train stopped at Dehra Dun, the northern valley town then part of western Uttar Pradesh and now the capital of a new state, Uttarakhand. The station, small and neat, wore an air of quiet and peaceful welcome. I exulted in it, waiting for the hills.

We got into a taxi. It sped so quickly through the markets of the town that I missed seeing the Shivalik Hills, the abode of Lord Shiva. Soon the Himalayas loomed in front of us, and Mussoorie spread on the mountain tops like a pendant.

We reached the town in the early hours of the morning, the driver negotiating carefully through the mist. I couldn't speak. I didn't know what to say. I clung to Ash's arm, looking out at the mountains, seeing way beyond them into a dream without end.

"We will stay in an old style hotel near Charleville. I

want to hear the rain on the tin roof, Ash." He readily agreed but strongly objected to our going in a rickshaw. "Da, I can't have this wizened old pahari carrying me. It's not right. Let's take a cab."

"Ash, you are depriving this man of his only livelihood. He's wizened but strong. Look, at his eyes. He's listening with hope."

"Fine, he'll take our luggage in the rickshaw and we'll walk along with him."

I was more than happy to walk along the hill road, through the mist, to our destination. The road was quiet with just a few locals and pink-cheeked Tibetan children walking, mingling effortlessly with the natural surroundings, the trees, the sky, the earth, the July drizzle and the mist. At the back of my mind, young, unsure, I hoped that I would not bump into anyone from home. The training academy for the new batch of Civil Services probationers was close by. It could have happened but it didn't.

Yet, sometimes, things that are done suddenly and out of character fall into place. Like the fragment of a wandering star that eventually finds its way.

The hotel had very few guests. By the time we had had our tea and washed, the room had been heated and water bottles warmed our four-poster bed. Ash held me close for a long time and then, and then it happened all at once. That was the first time we made love. It wouldn't have happened if I had not had those guilty pangs in Delhi and confessed them to the one and only Urvashi over the telephone. In her inimitable style she replied, eating her third aloo ka paratha in her sultry Kanpur verandah, "Yes, my cousin Kamini also felt very guilty when she let her husband touch her on her suhaag raat because she didn't love him at all. She married him because her ailing father and ambitious mother forced her to. Yeah, she slept with a man she didn't love and is continuing to do so for the roof above her head and a mindless life of security and comfort. SHE should feel guilty. What is your problem, my dear?" That did it! That was when I actually packed and left for Ash's place.

The rain kept pattering on the tin roof like a million nervous fingers as we slept in each other's arms. In the evening we walked up to the mandir on the craggy hill-top beside the silent palace. Ash stood in front of the beautiful idols of Radha Krishna and with folded hands he fell into a quiet prayer. I sat on the parapet and prayed too, letting the sky, the mountains, the earth and the wind pervade my whole being till I was nullified and become one with God. We sat for a long time together, watching the lights of Mussoorie come on one by one like diamonds on a diva's gown.

The next morning while we were walking back after a sumptuous breakfast in Company Bagh, we passed pretty cottages that tumbled down the hill like fallen toys. One cottage caught my eye and my mind locked it in its memory. It sat at the bottom of the hillock so snugly, its red tin roof atop cream walls and windows with lace curtains. It seemed to radiate and glow with peace and joy. The man who had a small store on the roadside said that the cottage had belonged to some Angrez family once upon a time and that was why it is called 'lyn'. Apparently a brook still existed right at the bottom of the hill, its size diminishing because of tree felling, its hill song silenced now by noise pollution. Lynn is a Celtic word for brook,

I learnt later. The collage was called Lynwood and next to it were Lynhurst, Lyneden and Lynregis and above on another hill, Lyndale we were told.

I told Ash that maybe, one day we could build a cottage like this one and call it – Lynmist. He smiled and said "You love the mist don't you?" and putting his arm around my shoulder he kissed my forehead so gently it hurt.

As we walked along the sun-splashed road, my mind was throbbing with so many thoughts revolving around just one wish: how to prolong this happiness, this exquisite and fragile time that will soon pass.

I said, "Can we spend the next two days in … ?"

"Landour? Yes, Da I just feel it's a super idea and we must simply go ahead with the plan. You know I was waiting for you to suggest it."

"I was scared to say it, but not now."

"Scared?"

"Yes." Thank God, he didn't ask for explanations, he seldom did.

You explain only when you aren't sure.

8

That night a funny kind of fear crept into my heart. I was speechless and numb trying to ward it off. Fortunately we were sitting at Whispering Windows restaurant listening to music so it seemed as if I was silent because I was enjoying the melody. We walked back, swaying a little and singing, "How many miles must a white dove fly before it can sleep in the sand." The wind rushing through the trees replied, "Soon." and Ash asked, "Can you hear that?" I lied, "No," and clung to him more tightly. That night I made love with an ardour and aggression that startled both him and me. He fell asleep soon after. I didn't, I didn't until dawn stole into the room on quiet feet.

As I said Landour was originally just a cantonment area in the late nineteenth century. During the 1970s it was not as developed as it is now. There were no hotels of merit so we checked into a small private lodging house near Char Dukan. It was a two-storied stone house with a tin roof, which must have been a comforting red once. Inside, it was shabby and musty too but the pots of geranium placed neatly in front of it more than made up for all the inadequacies. Like a true hill girl I revelled in that simple splendour.

Char Dukan, with its four little shops in a row and an even littler post office in between, was, to me, as breathtaking as ever. I felt as I did when I first saw it, I felt as if I had reached home.

After delicious cups of ginger tea we strolled along the road that sliced through the forest of deodars. We strolled along as the fragrance of wet earth assailed our senses and the colour of another day ending wrenched our hearts.... It was a spectacular sunset: the kind that one saw only in the hills after an afternoon shower. I thought of Shillong and my family, my childhood and my old school friends and, suddenly, I was crying. Ash hugged me tight, kissing my hair, asking no questions.

A voice, all of a sudden, slurred, "One shouldn't cry before it's time to cry. One shouldn't sit here before it's time to rest." Startled, we turned. On the wall opposite an old tramp sat. "My name is Anthony – I am not a ghost." he cackled, "Tell me, why are you sitting near the graveyard?" I jumped.

"Why are you?" Ash replied in a question.

"For the same reason as you guys," Anthony answered, lighting a Charminar.

"And what is that?" Ash continued, his eyes twinkling.

"I don't know," was the reply. "I beg your pardon, Anthony?"

"I don't know, that's the answer, the best answer of all." We stared at him as he hobbled away, chuckling.

We walked away too, in the opposite direction and went to a little shop glowing with life and the most amazing assortment of cheeses.

We picked up some Cheddar and wove our way back to the lodging house as the wind raced through the trees making us shiver and hold each other close, our hearts melting into one. We could see Landour's most famous resident, Ruskin Bond, walking a little ahead of us. I was, however, so stingy with the time I could spend with Ash that I let the moment pass. I was actually scared that Ashwin would catch up with Ruskin and spend some time with him. Ash just smiled at me; he understood.

Back in our little room I lit a tall red candle and placed it on the center table. In an old, freshly-washed Quink inkbottle I put a bunch of mountain daisies and sat it at the foot of the candle. Ash opened the Italian wine we had purchased in Delhi and poured it into the two wine glasses he had brought up with him. He placed them side by side on the table, the wine matching the colour of the elegant candle perfectly, while the mountain daisies of pink and white complemented our feelings of love – pure, fragile, and ephemeral. "Dear God," I prayed, "don't let him say anything. I don't want this moment to be overshadowed by words." God heard my prayers because Ashwin simply raised his glass to his lips and touched my glass and sipped.

Love poured out of me naturally and in abundance, as we lounged in that old sofa, drinking wine, eating cheese and singing old love songs … The first time ever I saw your face, Help me make it through the night, Yesterday, I am I said, Just call out my name and soon I will be there.

I lived my dreams through songs, knowing that they are but dreams and just songs.

The following day it poured incessantly, all day. We stayed in bed chatting, watching the rain, listening to it, savouring the fragrance of the earth through the empty window. Holding hands and with my head on his shoulder we recounted silly happy incidents of the past. The landlady served us what she'd cooked in her kitchen. Red hill rice and a vegetable gruel spiced with the typical Garhwali herb jakhia. It was delicious. We ate and slept. In the evening it cleared into yet another sunset of different shades of orange and pink, blue and grey, purple and mauve.

Then the sky deepened and another day was gone.

9

The last morning was, yes, misty and we walked up to the knoll where we'd first met. It was a dream like no other dream, a morning like no other morning, a feeling unsurpassed, a song beyond music and words, eternal and exquisite, "I wonder what Anthony would say if he saw us sitting here?" I asked Ash. He laughed, so happily, and replied, "I don't know because I don't know. Gosh! Da, it's really quite on answer. It does make life so simple."

"Naturally, Ashwin Kapur," I whispered, "because it is the truth. We do not know. We are forever seeking answers.

That's life." He laughed again. I had never seen him laugh as much as he did ever since Anthony imparted his special wisdom.

Like love, you sometimes find Truth in unusual places.

Somewhere in the lower slopes I could hear the tinkling of cowbells and the barking of dogs as the mist began to rise faster and faster to envelop us completely. Whenever I danced or laughed my mind would stop ticking. It would become free of thought and emotions, totally blank, leaving me refreshed afterwards. That was how I felt enclosed within that misty world, totally blank, at peace as if in meditation. We sat until the mist cleared and the sun slowly filtered in and then became unbearably strong. Our throats were parched and our stomachs ached with hunger. We sat because we didn't know so much time had passed.

At Char Dukan, we ate a huge breakfast of omelette sandwiches washed down with apple juice followed by tea and a plate of hot pakodas. Back in our room we packed slowly and with heavy hearts. In an empty plastic bag I put the mountain daisies that had adorned the table the night before. Into an empty matchbox I emptied the handful of earth I had brought from the knoll in a big leaf lying on the wayside. I emptied the room of all the memories and tucked them where no one can touch them for ... for no one should ever know where someone treasures love.

All that went into my baggage before we left the room and went down to meet the landlady to pay and say goodbye. "Very good couple you two," she gushed. "Good mix, na? Thai and English, very good, very good. Come again with your children okay?" I smiled and waved, "Thai and English." Ash chuckled under his breath while

I gave a last look and smiled at the geraniums bursting with life and joy. Then we caught the bus back to Delhi. I remember nothing of that journey because it rained all the way and I could have been anywhere, just about anywhere and nowhere.

I felt safe in the nowhereness. I revelled in it.

10

Back in Delhi the days passed quickly. The college was buzzing with activity: Freshers' Night, the Miss Indraprastha College contest, new teachers, new classes, the sweltering heat and flooded roads. I was part of everything yet a creature apart, thriving in my own new-found life. Arti, Sushma and Urvashi pulled my leg and barraged me with questions. "Enjoy the joy, the pain, the tears, the laughter. You are looking wonderful. Thank you Alain Delon," my friends chorused.

One has to, however, pay a price for everything. If you possess anything very precious it also means living with the constant fear of losing it. Unless one has the strength to accept that one can never ever possess anything or anyone. Thus I would, in those days, swim with the tide and against it. As much as I could I tried to be brave.

Ash had finished his work in Delhi by the time the heat had dissipated and the weather had mellowed into autumn. Leaves were falling from the trees, dancing down with the wind, as we walked hand in hand in Lodhi Gardens. We sat beside on old monument watching, talking while he smoked and I took a surreptitious drag once in a while. It was on such a day in September – just before university closed for the Dusherra-Diwali break – that he told me his next move. "I spoke with my publisher in London, Da, and he suggested that I rewrite the manuscript as a collection of essays, human interest stories. He feels that many more people will read it and benefit from it if it is presented in this way. I plan to move to England in November and work on it. I will also do some interviews there. After meeting people here I realized that parenting, the agony and the ecstasy, is a universal problem and the future is there waiting like a rattlesnake for everyone, everywhere." It was only then, after a whole year had gone by, that I asked him why he chose the topic.

"I didn't choose the topic, the topic chose me. After my mother succumbed to cancer and left us forever, I realized how much she had actually given to the four of us. Father gave us next to nothing. He paid our school and college fees, put food on the table and paid the huge, unwieldy staff that he enjoyed having around. My mamas and mamis gave my mother the necessary support whenever needed: when there were issues of health, discipline, academic problems, during the days of tears and smiles, they were there. Dad would carry on with his work and travel and hectic social life. Any spare time was spent with his mother who lived in another wing of the house. She had her own life totally separate from us – very similar to Dad's. I always felt that if he had had siblings and not inherited all of his father's timber business he would have been a more balanced person. Mom seemed to have loved him all the same. Amazing! Anyway, Da, let's not talk about it. It's so painful and infuriating that's why I had to write the book. Arjun is playing golf and tennis, excelling in both. Anjali is happily married – I think. Anasuya is dead, an overdose ... and I don't want to talk about it. It happened soon after Ma passed away. Da, I have to go. I have to finish the book."

You have to finish what you started. That's part of the ride.

11

A few days before Diwali the festival of lights, he flew to London. One of his cousins from Shimla, on a visit to Delhi, was also there to see him off. The four of us from college along with Raveena, waved him farewell with bouquets of flowers and good wishes and love. Then he was gone. I was grateful that Ashwin had often mentioned Raveena and, consequently, I learnt that she was very reserved. Otherwise I would have thought that her coolness was due to the fact that I was from the Northeast and, therefore, not a suitable 'bhabhi'. We parted warmly, sharing a common love.

Before he left I made him promise that we would not communicate for the one year that we'd be apart. It upset him enormously and he just stared at me for a long time trying to understand. "I will be able to cope only if I just tuck this whole thing away for a year. Believe me, this is the only way," I said before he could say anything. It was at a quiet dinner at his barsati terrace with the hum of the traffic below and that November nip in the air that heralded a much-awaited winter. Delhi was coming alive while within me life had come to a standstill.

12

The months flew and in April-May our final exams commenced and ended. By the end of June I was a graduate.

Knowing that Saihun would soon be going to the US to pursue her studies, I decided to stay home with my parents. I joined Loreto Convent as an English teacher, officiating for a senior staff member who had taken leave. That was when I realized I would like to spend the rest of my life teaching.

Very quickly another November was approaching. School closed and the winter set in. In March I resumed my teaching and enjoyed my classes enormously. The children, ever curious and mischievous, diverted my mind during the day and in the evenings I corrected their exercise books, their delightful essays scented with innocence and hope.

In this simple act I found great comfort.

13

There are so many coincidences in life that occur to tie up lost threads, broken threads in the strange fabric of life. In June the teacher resumed her duties and Sai was going to school to collect her results and certificates and my parents asked me to accompany her. I was only too happy to do so. I was longing to be on the move again. Besides, I had received the most wonderful news from our go between, Arti, that Ashwin was returning mid-March. I gave her the equally good news that I was going to be in Mussoorie during that period. I couldn't quite believe that the whole thing was fitting in so well. That was the time I should have guessed but I didn't. Instead, inside, I was singing and dancing … all the way to Delhi and to Mussoorie in that very same train that I had travelled in with Ashwin over a year ago.

14

It was the tenth of June and I had checked into the hotel, into the same room with the same bottle of wine, Italian it was and bought from the same shop in Delhi, on the way up. In an old Quink bottle, the same Quink bottle, I arranged mountain daisies. Arti had called two days back to inform me that he should be landing by midnight and he would take a taxi from the airport and come straight to Mussoorie, to the Carlton. After seeing Saihunlang and her Delhi-bound friends off, I went back to the hotel and slept.

It was almost dusk and outside my room tired birds hummed their tired songs. I woke up for dinner and tried to call Arti but her maid said the whole family had gone out. I tried again after midnight and was given the same information, a little hesitantly. I should have guessed then too but I didn't. Instead I put on some music and waltzed all over the room on the old carpet. After a while I slept again.

It was much after dawn when I heard voices whispering outside my room. I jumped out of bed and opened the door to face three ashen faces. "Folks, what's up?" I needn't have asked but I did because I was sad. I knew … and I was sad. "A plane crash?" I heard myself ask. Urvashi was too devastated to talk. Ashen-faced she stared at me, sorrow swirling in her deep dark eyes. Arti held me as Sushma spoke, "No, Da, oh! Da, it was a car crash in London on the way to the airport. That is what the person who called said, his brother I think."

I don't remember what happened after that but I do remember telling my friends to come with me to Landour, to the hilltop where Ashwin and I first met. That I remember and there I recited one of my favourite pieces from Tagore.

"*I think I shall stop startled if ever we meet after our next birth, walking in the light of the faraway world. I shall know those eyes then as morning stars and yet feel that they have belonged to some unremembered evening sky of a former life. I shall know that the magic of your face is not all its own but has stolen the passionate light that was in my eyes at some immemorial meeting ... and then gathered from my love a mystery that has now forgotten its origin.*"

The lines flowed out like a river in spate.

The tournament was almost over when Dalinia asked for the car. After tidying herself and arranging her thoughts and her expression appropriately she got into her car and left. She arrived in time for the prize distribution ceremony. In time to be seated right next to her husband. In time for people to notice and for photographers to click pictures. Arjun Kapur won the trophy and it was but natural for everyone including Dalinia to go up to him. So when the crowd had thinned and the air had cleared she walked up and congratulated him, after which she quickly added,

"I knew your brother, Ashwin."

"Really ?"

"Yes ... during my college days. He, he ... died so tragically."

"I know. I was there."

A brief silence passed by and then glided away guiltily, an unwanted intruder.

"Tell me about it ... did he suffer, did he say anything, did..?"

"A van crashed into our car, it was on a curve and the driver lost control ..."

"And then?"

"He died on the way to the hospital, the medical attendants in the ambulance did all they could to revive him but they couldn't."

"Did he ... say anything like ... "

"Now that you ask, yes, in fact he kept repeating one line till the end."

"May I say those lines?"

And before he could reply she looked straight at him and whispered,

"There is no such place as far away."

Then she was gone, moving amidst the happy crowd as the memory sailed away like a kite.